D0407341

TUBBY MEETS KATRINA

TUBBY MEETS KATRINA

A Tubby Dubonnet Novel by

TONY DUNBAR

NewSouth Books
Montgomery | Louisville

NewSouth Books
P.O. Box 1588
Montgomery, AL 36102

Library of Congress Cataloging-in-Publication Data

Dunbar, Anthony P.
Tubby meets Katrina : a Tubby Dubonnet novel / by Tony Dunbar.
p. cm.
ISBN-13: 978-1-58838-203-0
ISBN-10: 1-58838-203-6
1. Attorney and client--Fiction. 2. Hurricane Katrina, 2005--Fiction.
3. Louisiana--Fiction. I. Title.
PS3554.U46336T83 2006
813'.54--dc22

2006008581

Design by Randall Williams
Printed in the United States of America

This novel is a work of fiction. All the names, characters, and settings are purely
imaginary. There is no Tubby Dubonnet, and the real New Orleans is different from his
make-believe city.

For Hugh Knox, a *gude man*,
and always for Mary Price

Tubby Meets Katrina

1

TWO SHEETS TO THE WIND, THE NIGHT JAILER AT THE Oldroads, Louisiana, Pointe Croupee Parish Jail castled his rook and his king. He had been playing chess with a state inmate named Bonner Rivette for the past three nights, and his score was one win, six losses. Playing games with the prisoners was against the rules, but this jail was beyond boring after midnight. The staff wasn't even supposed to watch television. Tonight the jailer had actually chugged a couple of beers in the Circle K parking lot on his way to work. He knew that was against the rules, too, but this place was driving him stir crazy.

Bonner, the prisoner, happened to be a night owl, and he sat up reading old paperbacks until he found out the guard liked to play chess. The guard knew that Rivette was a convicted murderer, and he placed no stock in Rivette's claim to be innocent. He also knew Rivette was here because he had won a retrial, and they had bused him back from Angola so he could see the same judge again. Good old Isaac Crane, His Honor, hadn't liked Bonner the first time around. This boy had sliced up his sister and the Church of God pastor, really bad, all in one "sudden emotional explosion," a psychologist said, over the issue of who got to drive a Toyota station wagon. The pastor had lingered but eventually he died.

The guard remembered all this because when he had been a senior in high school this was the biggest thing that had ever happened in Pointe Croupee Parish, and his own cousin had once dated Rivette's sister even though she went to Morganza Christian Academy and the cousin went to River Parish Regional.

The excuse for the retrial was that a state psychiatrist, not the one who had testified at trial, had said that Bonner Rivette was an extremely anti-social psychotic who had no normal mental faculties at the time of the crime. The psychiatrist had a high school guidance counselor's notes to support this theory. Yet the county attorney had filed the report in the wastebasket and never told Bart Crookedhawk, a recent law school graduate appointed by the same Judge Crane to defend the indigent Rivette, anything about it. That was called concealing exculpatory evidence.

But now District Court Judge Crane had the flu, and that was why Bonner Rivette's retrial had been delayed and why he was still in the parish jail.

Rivette, long curly brown hair and a deeply lined face for a young man in his twenties, looked intently at the chess board balanced on a folding chair outside the bars of his cage. The cell block smelled strongly of Pine-Sol and urine. The guard's brown uniform was crisply, annoyingly, pressed.

The prisoner moved his pawn and captured the guard's black bishop.

"Aw, shoot." The guard's mouth dropped open in mock despair before he grinned and brayed, "You just gave me your queen!"

He leaned forward triumphantly and lifted his horse delicately by the ears. Holding it like a dainty teacup the guard lightly flicked his man against his opponent's piece. Without hesitating Rivette whipped a towel around the guard's neck and roped it through the bars. He twisted it hard to cut off the air supply. The guard knocked over the chess set trying to make a noise and get to his can of pepper spray. Bonner kicked through the bars at the guard's fingers and tried to knee him in the groin, all the while twisting the noose tighter.

When it was over the guard was lying unconscious and barely breathing on the concrete floor. His prisoner reached through the bars to steal the keys from the motionless officer's belt and unlock the cell door. He snuck out silently and loped down the hall. Another jailer was snoring at his desk up front. Rivette opened one door, which creaked but didn't wake the guard. He tiptoed across the room, and slipped out another door to the street.

It was a small, hot Louisiana bed-and-breakfast town. Rivette knew it well. It was one of many his family had passed through chasing the oil drilling business. There were two traffic lights. At one end of the strip a neon sign blinked MI   LOEB. Even that light was too much. Rivette slunk around the jail building and ran down the empty street in the direction of darkness. There would be at least one police car somewhere, and he planned to avoid it. He ran from bleak alley to cherry laurel hedge to carport until he got away from civilization, out to where the doublewides are parked way off in the cotton fields. The night was pitch black except for a sliver of moon. The criminal took off jogging down the highway.

2

TUBBY DUBONNET HAD JUST GOTTEN OFF A PLANE FROM Bolivia the Saturday night before Hurricane Katrina hit, and until his feet touched down on Concourse D of the Louis Armstrong International Airport in New Orleans he had not even heard about the darn thing. But there it was, a red-tipped, yellow, organic swirl on CNN, like a cheerleader's flounced pom-pom and about as big as the screen. It was proceeding north through the Gulf of Mexico at a leisurely twenty miles an hour, and New Orleans was right in the middle of the forecaster's cone. Tubby lingered to stare at the hypnotic image. The wheel spun slowly counter-clockwise. The weary traveler yawned and went to collect his baggage downstairs.

This happens every year. Grin and bear it.

The familiar heat hit him when he exited the air conditioned terminal, and he quickly flagged a cab to take him to his house Uptown. All of his daughters were gone. The place would be empty. Yet it would be strange and wonderful to be home at last. Five months in Bolivia, the scene of so many events needing to be forgotten, was plenty. Now that Tubby's fears of being indicted by a federal grand jury in matters relating to the Cowappatack

Tribal Casino were less immediate, he had decided that Louisiana was the safest and best place to be.

Labor strife in Santa Cruz had almost prevented him from boarding his airplane for home. Barricades and burning barrels lit the streets of this prosperous metropolis, and various governmental officials were hanging in effigy from the tree limbs in the public squares. Big men and women sporting derby hats stared menacingly at him from behind the flames as his taxi driver honked through, humming a revolutionary vallenato pop hit by Carlos Vives.

"Es is okay for you are leaving today," the driver announced. Tubby agreed with that.

Fourteen hours later he was in a United Cab rocking along the I-10 toward downtown New Orleans. All this driver wanted to talk about was the coming hurricane, but it still didn't sink in with Tubby.

"See all those cars?" The cabdriver gestured to the outgoing lanes, which were filled with bumper-to-bumper traffic. "They all got the sense to evacuate. This is gonna be the big one, they say."

"Really?" The lawyer was bushed from his flight. "It's called Katrina, right?"

"Means cleansing hand," the driver informed him. He was a young guy, wearing heavy black-framed glasses and a baseball cap backwards. It advertised Ezra Brooks Bourbon. Tubby figured him for a UNO student. "That's what the internet says."

"Well, I hope it cleanses the Yucatan Peninsula instead of us. Not that I wish any ill . . ."

"They say it's coming right here, though, tomorrow night."

"Why are you around then?" Tubby yawned again. He was ready for bed.

"My girlfriend is supposed to sing for mass in church tomorrow morning. We're staying here anyhow. We're in an old house in Mid-City. It stood up to Camille so I guess it can stand up to this."

"Camille? Betsy was the one hit here."

"Whichever. I wasn't born yet. But the house was built in 1920. I know cause it's been in the family, and it never had any trouble before now."

"Same with me," Tubby said. Of course you always had to take hurricanes seriously, but this one was still twenty-four hours away. Its trajectory would likely change. The projections would all be different by morning. It was way too early to worry about this particular storm, much less pack up and leave town.

If you did leave you'd be caught for days in traffic. Tubby didn't need that. He needed a drink and a good night's sleep. Living in South America was a demanding experience. Good or bad, he couldn't yet say. He was just happy to be back in the Big Easy, in the Bayou State, in the "Sportsman's Paradise," in the good ol' US of A.

Speeding down the Interstate, this was one of those times he wished he had a cell phone. If he had a cell phone he could call his daughters while riding in this taxi. Having been out of the country for so long he craved human contact. But if he had a cell phone his ex-wife or his clients would call him whenever they felt like it, and Tubby had always valued as many buffers from the world as possible.

The taxi deposited him in front of his house. It was dimly illuminated by streetlights obscured within the live oak trees that shaded the entire block. The driver helped him with his luggage as far as the sidewalk and accepted his pay. "Good luck," he called as he sped off.

"Same to you," Tubby said. Good luck? For what? Oh, right, the hurricane.

His house keys remained where he had hidden them under one of the flagstones on the walkway laid across an unruly monkey-grass lawn. Crickets hummed outside. The air was hot and sweet. He savored the magnolia-scented aroma of his city. The keys were a little wet and dirty, but worked the door just fine.

Thanks to its many cracks and drafts, the house did not even smell as though it had been closed up for months. The lights came on when he flipped the switch, which was one major improvement over Bolivia. His next-door neighbor had been collecting the mail, but that could wait until tomorrow. Right now, let's see what there is to drink.

Tubby sat in the kitchen, savoring a large bourbon over old ice. The neighborhood seemed quieter than he remembered. Maybe he had better check in on the kids.

They weren't really kids. The oldest, Debbie, was married and had a baby. Second came Christine, the wisest, who had just begun her sophomore year at Tulane, Tubby's alma mater, the week before. The youngest and least pegged, Collette, still lived six blocks away with her mother, Mattie, Tubby's ex. None of them had officially lived with him for about ten years, not since the divorce. He picked up the phone.

"Daddy!" Christine screamed. "Where are you?" There was loud music in the background.

"Right here in New Orleans, at the house. I'm back home."

"When did you get here?"

He told her.

"Don't you know there's a hurricane coming? Everybody else is leaving."

"I didn't know about it till I got here just a little while ago. Where are your sisters?"

"Collette and Mom are in Disney World in Orlando with

some of Collette's friends from school. They are supposed to come back tomorrow night, but now I don't know. Debbie and Marcus and the baby drove up to Uncle Harold's in Hattiesburg this afternoon. He said he had plenty of room."

Probably because his girlfriend left him, Tubby thought. "What about you?" he inquired.

"Tulane closed the whole campus yesterday. Everybody had to get out of the dorms. They've got a bus taking kids to Jackson, Mississippi, tomorrow if they don't have anywhere else to go."

"Why don't you come over here to the house?"

"They say there might be twenty feet of water Uptown, Daddy. You've got to leave, too."

"I'll see about that tomorrow," her father said wearily. "You think you'll take the Tulane bus?"

"Possibly. Brent is thinking about staying at his mother's apartment on Spain Street in the Marigny. It's on the second floor."

Hmmm, Brent was her boyfriend, a junior and pre-med student. Tubby had only met him briefly before departing for Bolivia. There was something about him Tubby didn't like, couldn't say exactly what except he had never been especially fond of any of the girls' boyfriends.

"Where's Brent's mother?"

"I'm sure she'll be there, too. She never leaves for anything."

"Perhaps you should get out of town on the Tulane bus," Tubby repeated. "Sounds like it could be fun." Lots more fun than staying with Brent.

She ignored him. "It's great to hear your voice, Daddy. When was the last time you called?"

"Last month, wasn't it? On your birthday?"

"That was two months ago."

"Yeah, sure. But did you get my letters?"

"I got a cute little postcard of some furry pig."

"That's actually a rodent called a capybaras, and people eat them. They have a couple at the Audubon Zoo."

"Yuck. Tell me about your trip."

He didn't take the offer seriously. The music was getting louder. "I'd like to. Maybe we could have lunch tomorrow and . . ."

"Don't forget about the hurricane, Daddy."

"Right. Well, in a day or two, after this all blows over, let's get together."

"Okay. Is everything all right?"

"Great. Everything's fine. All I need is a good night's sleep in my own bed."

"Let's talk tomorrow, so I know where you are."

"You can bet I'll be right here."

"Okay. Good night. I love you."

"Love you, too."

So he was alone in a quiet house. And he was beat. Tubby freshened up his drink and dragged himself upstairs.

3

BONNER RIVETTE WAS SUCCESSFULLY ESCAPING FROM JAIL. Walking though cottonfields near the False River, he kept his eyes on the distant horizon revealing itself in the dawn of another hot day. He knew this trick—pick a faraway landmark and keep right at it while you're covering the miles. Don't waste time walking in circles. He jumped an irrigation ditch and stepped on cabbages. He saw a distant combine stirring the morning mist. He hit a blacktop road near a sign for Louisiana 984. He carefully looked both ways. It was an east/west road, and he wanted to go south. Hearing a vehicle approach he jumped into the rows of dirt clods and dewy vegetables to hide. He watched a chinch bug crawl by his nose. A pickup roared past in a cloud of dust. Rivette waited a minute and got up.

He dusted himself off, sniffed the air, and crossed the road. Then he set off through the next field. There were big sweat stains on his navy blue T-shirt and navy blue sweat pants. Jail garb. He loped along in Ho Chi Minh sandals made from a thrown-away car tire and plastic bags he had twisted into strings. He had discarded the jail's official brown brogans the first chance he got. He wiped the sweat from his face and marched across wet row after row of late summer crops. His hair was matted over his prison-pale forehead. There was a wild grin of freedom on his face.

TUBBY AWOKE MUCH LATER than his customary 5:30 AM. It was more like 10 o'clock. He brushed his teeth, got dressed, and made his way downstairs. He had the coffeemaker working when he flipped on the television and saw Katrina again. Man, was that sucker ever big! The satellite photograph showed it literally covering the whole Gulf of Mexico. It was still about twelve hours from landfall, the announcer said. Plenty of time for a course change, but it still looked like it was headed straight for New Orleans.

He flipped the channels. More of the same—all the local channels, the weather channel, and CNN were full of Katrina. Some of the cable channels had game shows, church services and old movies, but none was quite as engaging as watching this monster weather formation rotate around in the hot waters of the Gulf.

Tubby went outside for the newspaper, but it wasn't there. He reminded himself to call the carrier and resume delivery. His street was alive with motorists, however. He saw his neighbors loading their cars. He ambled next door, to Chad Rouseau's house. Rouseau had been collecting Tubby's mail, and right now he was nailing plywood over his sunroom windows.

"Good morning, Chad."

"Hey, you're back. I've got a lot of stuff for you. Just give me a minute and I'll go get it."

Tubby offered to lend him a hand and together they got the plywood nailed over a window frame.

"This is getting to be a habit," Rouseau said. "Twice already this season. You gonna board your place up?"

"I should, but I've never done that." One reason was that it was hard to nail plywood over eighteen windows and doors, eight of them being close to thirty feet off the ground. Another reason was it seemed to him that the plywood was unlikely to make a difference. Winds high enough to blow out glass might just as easily tear off the roof. Maybe he was just too lazy for the job.

"Are you going to leave?" Chad asked. This was getting to be the standard question.

"No, I don't plan to. What about you?"

"I'm going over to my sister's in Lafayette as soon as I finish up here. I'm driving out Highway 90 on the West Bank because the I-10 is filling up fast. The news just said the mayor's going to declare a mandatory evacuation around noon."

"Wow. That's a first."

They got the plywood up, and Chad brought Tubby a big brown Langenstein's grocery bag full of mail.

"Good luck on your drive," Tubby said.

"Same to you. We'll all probably be back tomorrow."

Tubby carried the sack of mail back to the house. He poured himself a cup of coffee and idly picked through the stuff to ascertain that it was largely junk. On television, the big storm was still making its slow circle in the Gulf.

It made you nervous, the way it kept turning around and around and getting closer. Tubby put the mail aside and decided it was time to retrieve his car. The Chrysler was not in his driveway, unfortunately, but at a gas station down on Magazine Street where, over the last few months, they had basically overhauled his entire engine and installed new brakes all around. He had spoken to Max, the mechanic just last week. It had been an expensive long-distance call, but worth it. Max said the car was all done and running great. He would have it gassed up and ready when Tubby showed up to claim it.

Good for him that the station was open on Sundays.

But when Tubby got there he found it wasn't open after all. A cardboard sign hung over one of the pumps. "Sorry. Out of

Gas." And there was Tubby's Chrysler, sitting parked in the lot and polished, just like Max said it would be. The only problem was that it was hemmed in between a dumpster and the wall of the garage, and its forward motion was blocked by an enormous green GMC Yukon. This was typical of the massive cars preferred by the women of the neighborhood for carrying their children to school.

Tubby had a key and could get into his own car, which he did. It roared to life at the merest tap on the switch, but the Yukon was in front and a wooden fence was behind. Tubby got out to inspect. The fence was actually built atop a foot-tall concrete block foundation. Getting rid of that would require a sledge hammer. He looked inside the smoked windows of the Yukon. The doors were definitely locked. When he jerked on one, the car alarm went off.

Whoop, Whoop, Wheep, Wheep. It echoed up and down the street. Tubby waited patiently in front of the gas station. He expected management, the car owner, or the police to respond quickly to the alarm. After ten minutes the noise finally stopped. No one had showed up. Tubby reached the conclusion that his Chrysler was not going to take him anywhere today.

There was an emergency number taped to the inside of the station's door, and Tubby memorized it. He walked home where he would find the nearest phone. But that number didn't give satisfaction either. It just rang. Now it was past noon, and the TV news was a little more alarming. In a press conference that morning, the mayor had told everybody to leave the city. The Superdome had been opened as a "shelter of last resort," and reporters were interviewing the people who were beginning to stream out of the French Quarter, pulling luggage on wheels and clutching pillowcases stuffed with their possessions. Here were two Dutch students, giddy with being young and on an adventure, who had been in town for only two days.

"The hotel is closing, and we will be fine," the girl with long blonde hair told the camera confidently, flashing a blinding North Sea smile.

"How have you liked New Orleans so far?" the reporter asked her male companion.

"It is very hot here," he laughed, "but we love it so well."

Aerial footage of the Interstate showed a sluggish river of cars. They crept along notwithstanding "counterflow" measures which pointed all lanes out of town.

Tubby finally started thinking hurricane. He looked into the pantry for bottled water and canned goods. He found red wine, liver pâté and cranberry sauce from Thanksgivings past.

He called Flowers.

Flowers was a resourceful man. He was Tubby's private detective and his friend. His real name was Sanré Fueres, but everyone called him Flowers.

"Yo," came the familiar voice.

"Hey, Flowers, this is Tubby."

"Where are you, boss?" Flowers shouted. "Stateside?"

"I'm here, at my house, without transportation."

"You want to stay? You want to leave town? I got transportation."

"What are you doing?"

"I'm here for the duration. My agency is under contract to guard the Petrofoods Helicopters field in Kenner. They moved their personnel and most of their stuff over to their base in Lafayette. There's just a few choice items here. I've got a crane, I've got a truck, I've got . . ."

"Can you pick me up?"

"Sure. You want to grab your stuff? Then hike over to Claiborne Avenue and meet me on the neutral ground."

The neutral ground? What's that all about?

TUBBY DUMPED OUT his green flight bag, which was full of dirty clothes from Bolivia and the talons of an unspecified predatory bird, a souvenir he had purchased from a stall at the Santa Cruz airport. He raided his dresser and stuffed in some clean underwear, pants, and a shirt. He reached into the bottom drawer and extricated a handgun. It was a Smith & Wesson .45, still in its original black leather holster, an old weapon from an earlier time. He stared at it carefully, turning it over in his hand, before he put it in his pack. The lawyer did not normally carry a gun. He didn't believe in violence.

Walking downstairs he passed the framed photograph of his three daughters, taken at Debbie's graduation from high school. He touched it, paused, and considered whether he should take it along. Descending the stair wall were other framed pictures: his parents, his grandparents, baby pictures of the girls. He couldn't take them all, so he left them there and continued on his way.

In the kitchen he looked for food. There was an opened bag of Fritos. He stuck that under his arm. A half-finished bottle of bourbon. He pushed that into his green bag. Behind *The Joy of Cooking* was a stack of twenty-dollar bills. He fanned that like a deck of cards and stuck it into the pocket of his jeans. Flight bag in one hand, sack of Fritos held between his teeth, he went out the front door, found his keys, and locked the place up. Off to Claiborne Avenue.

FLOWERS'S ARRIVAL in a C-12 Airodream helicopter on the wide gassy median between the lanes of Business Route 90, also known as Claiborne Avenue, would have attracted more attention had there been any people around. As it was, the city had become deserted this hot and sunny Sunday afternoon. There were lots of cars parked on the median, or neutral ground as locals referred to it, deposited there by owners hoping to avoid damage from the anticipated inundation of rain. After all, a typical summer storm in this neighborhood could put four inches of water in the streets, and a good hurricane might lay down a foot. The highest ground around was the city property in the middle of the street. Flowers had no trouble locating a big enough spot to land, however. The helicopter came down surprisingly easy, with plenty of satisfactory clatter, in front of Ursulines Academy which had just completed construction of a new gymnasium. On the other side of the Avenue, the churches might have had early services that morning, but they were boarded up now as if some dictator had outlawed all religious observance.

Flowers gestured for Tubby to climb aboard. The detective was wearing mirror sunglasses and looked as happy as a World War Two ace ready to down Jerries over London.

"Get in," he yelled, but the noise was too great to do more than read lips. The lawyer figured it out and lifted his slightly overweight self into the passenger side of the two-seater. Actually, there was another seat behind, but it was full of ropes and gear.

"Welcome to the Cajun Airforce," Flowers yelled. "Cocktails are four dollars." He didn't wait for Tubby to strap himself in before he yanked the stick and the helicopter swooped up into the air.

Claiborne Avenue, and Tubby's neighborhood, swiftly got smaller. What got larger was the Superdome and, as they soared west, the traffic jam still working itself out on the I-10.

"That's the long way to get to Houston," Flowers yelled, pointing at the cars.

Tubby's stomach wasn't feeling so great. "God, there's a lot of them," he said. The line of traffic stretched as far as the eye could see. "Where are we going?" he shouted.

"I was going to take you back to my base, but no hurry. Have you got someplace else you want to go?"

"I haven't seen my office in a long time."

"We can do that," Flowers said, and he maneuvered their craft into another big arc. The Superdome and the New Orleans skyline came back to the foreground, and rushed closer.

"Look at that." Flowers pointed off the side to the lines of refugees circling the football stadium.

"So many people," Tubby said. "What are they going to eat in there?"

"MREs, probably."

"What's that?"

"Meals Ready to Eat. The military and FEMA say they've got it all under control. Plenty of rations for everybody."

"How are we going to land at my building?"

"Right on top is the plan," Flowers said.

And he succeeded, gently dropping his Airodream into the circle painted on the roof of the forty-nine-story Place Palais.

He cut the engine, and as the blades gradually ran down the men relished the returning silence and lack of vibration. Tubby took a few deep breaths. They disembarked. It was a hot afternoon. The view of the city gripping the banks of the Mississippi River was spectacular. Tall clouds commanded the sky, however. Some had sharp claws like immense prehistoric birds, migrating westward, and the breeze was picking up.

"The clouds get darker the farther south you look," Tubby observed.

"Yep, it's coming in," Flowers said. He stood a lean six foot-five. Tubby was used to seeing him in a sports jacket, but Flowers looked pretty cool in jeans and a Perlis sports shirt marked with a crawfish. Tubby thought he personally looked pretty tough, too, facing the wind on top of this skyscraper, at least when he sucked in his gut.

"How the hell do you suppose we can get inside?" he asked.

"Let's see if Manuel is here." Flowers flipped open his cell phone and pressed the buttons. Tubby knew Manuel. He was the building's chief of security. Tubby gave him a fruit basket every year at Christmas. He didn't realize that Flowers knew him on a first-name basis.

Part of the conversation was in Spanish. The lawyer wasn't fluent, not by a long shot, but he had learned how to obtain life's necessities while in Bolivia mainly by watching the TV news and trying to follow what was happening in the world. The gist was Flowers's request to *"Abre la Puerta!"*

The detective closed his phone. "I'd be lost without this," he commented to himself.

"I still don't have one," Tubby said.

"No? You ought to. Take mine till the hurricane's over." He handed Tubby the compact stainless steel contraption.

"I wouldn't know what to do with it." Tubby turned the little machine over in his palm.

"You'll figure it out. I'll write the number down for you. I've got another one in my pocket and that's what my men call me on. It's unsafe for you to be out here without any communications."

The rusty metal door at the top of the staircase groaned open, and Manuel was there.

"Nice wheels," he said, admiring the helicopter.

"It gets you there in a hurry," Flowers said. "Mr. Dubonnet wants to see his office."

"The building is closed, but I will let you in. Please make your visit quick though because I am soon setting all of the alarms."

"Are you leaving?"

"No, I will be here. My family is gone back to Texas. But I'm staying here in the building. Maybe we can open back up for business tomorrow or Tuesday."

He led them down one flight of stairs to an elevator, which he summoned with his key and a plastic card. He pushed the button for the forty-third floor.

"You remembered," Tubby said happily.

"Sure, I know where your office is, Mr. Dubonnet. You been gone?"

"Yeah, five months almost, down to South America."

"Really, what country?"

"Bolivia."

"I have never been there. My family is from Nicaragua. We have only been north, never south. I have seen your secretary Cherrylynn many times. She comes to work while you are gone?"

"Oh, yes. That's quite all right. Cherrylynn has the run of the place." Thank goodness. Cherrylynn was the only one who knew what was going on most of the time. She was a single woman, a refugee from some relationship in the Great Northwest, and she was determined to carve out a life for herself without male assistance in New Orleans. She did, however, accept the assistance of a job with Tubby, and he knew that he received more from her than he paid for. She had also always had a crush on Flowers. Tubby had last spoken with her a week ago. He expected that Cherrylynn had taken herself off to somewhere safe. That girl could take care of herself.

The elevator doors opened, and there were the big glass doors with DUBONNET & ASSOCIATES printed in gold. There were not really any associates, since Tubby's last partner, Reggie Turntide, had met an unfortunate death years before, but it sounded better to have associates.

Tubby found that he was glad to see it all again. He had a key card for the doors.

"You guys can make yourselves at home," the attorney said as he walked through his reception area and into the corridor behind. The detective and security man shrugged. There wasn't much to do in a lawyer's office. Manuel took his leave. He told Flowers that the elevator would be open for him. They could get back to the roof the same way they came down.

"Just don't try to go to no other floors," he cautioned.

"*No problema,*" Flowers replied. He plopped himself down in Tubby's easy chair and opened a six-month-old *New Orleans CitiBusiness.*

Tubby walked to his office at the back. His desk was just as he had left it. The same files were on top. Even one marked Cowappatack Tribal Casino. He shuddered. That one was better shredded. But he didn't shred it or anything else. Instead he walked to his window with the panoramic view of the French Quarter and the majestic bend of the Mississippi River. The black clouds coming across the horizon from the direction of the Gulf of Mexico made the scene quite dramatic. His city looked just about the same as he remembered it, though. A towboat was pushing a string of barges slowly upriver. In the French Quarter, street lights were flickering on. It was a great city. He had missed it. Nowhere was life so sweet as in New Orleans. Nowhere could you find a better and more tolerant population. It had its problems, sure. New Orleans had its Bolivia-like absurdity and inefficiency. But people here contributed to life much more than they took away. Once this storm passed, he planned to spend some quality time rediscovering his city.

All of a sudden the idea of evacuating it now didn't seem to make much sense.

"Let's go," he told Flowers.

"That's it?" The detective uncurled from his chair and stretched.

"Yep. It's pretty much the way I left it, I'm happy to say."

They went into the outside hall, and Tubby locked up. "What

did you say my cell phone number is?" he asked Flowers.

Flowers told him again, and Tubby scribbled it on one of his cards, which he stuck in the crack of the door.

"Just for Cherrylynn," he said. "In case she shows up."

They took the elevator back to the roof.

"You can bunk down in Kenner with me," Flowers said when they reached the open air. "We've got a whole warehouse to call home. There's always room for one more."

"You know, I think I'll stay at my house. This may sound crazy, but I'd like to be there if our storm turns into something big. I appreciate the offer, but I've got a lot of stuff to look after."

"You already packed your bag." Flowers sounded disappointed and concerned.

"Yeah, but I changed my mind. I've been away so long, I just think I might stay to see what happens here. One night in my own bed just wasn't enough."

"Well, hell, boss, I've got to get this baby back to base. This wind is getting bad. I'm supposed to guard the plant. Otherwise I'd join you."

"Oh, that's okay. I'm not worried about this hurricane. In fact, while I've still got a little daylight, I'd kind of like to walk around. Do you suppose you could put me back on the street?" He was thinking, if I'm going to rediscover my city, why not do it now?

"On the street? We'll see."

They climbed aboard and Flowers started the big prop. With the flapping of a hundred mad condors, the Airodream lifted off.

"How far do you want to walk?" Flowers yelled.

"Just put me down the first place you see!" Tubby shouted back.

"How about right there?" Flowers pointed to the parking lot beside the Amtrak station. It was virtually empty.

Tubby made the okay sign with his fingers, and the big bird descended to asphalt. When they thumped down Tubby grabbed his green bag and jumped out.

"Don't forget you've got a phone," Flowers called through cupped hands. "Call me if you need anything. I don't know if I can take this up anymore in the wind, but we've got some big trucks that will just about go anywhere."

"Don't worry about me," Tubby mouthed. The helicopter lifted away. Why should anyone worry? I can take care of myself. I've got three intelligent daughters, and all of them have moved away to safety. Raisin Partlow, Tubby's running buddy, was still in Bolivia, as safe and sound as one could be in a country paralyzed by strikes. There's nobody else I'm responsible for, he thought. Let's enjoy a stroll, get back to the house, curl up with a fifth, and see if the Astros or Braves are on TV.

He hefted up his green bag, took a gulp of steamy air, paused for a brief cool breeze coming from somewhere, and set off for St. Charles Avenue.

It was kind of nice. Very few cars around, so he could jaywalk across Lee Circle. There were, however, a few family groups on the march, bearing plastic supermarket bags full of their stuff, pulling children along, all headed in the opposite direction toward downtown. Tubby stopped to help a lady lift her baby carriage over the curb.

"Where are y'all going?" he asked.

"The Superdome. We all be all right when we get there. Mr. Benson's got the hot dogs cooking."

"Sounds nutritious," Tubby said. He could use a hot dog himself right about now.

He saw a red streetcar clattering Uptown on St. Charles with a "Not in Service" sign on the front. He knew it was going to the Carrollton barn. The old green Perley-Thomas streetcars must already have been put away. It was always prudent to protect the antiques. A hot wind picked up as he proceeded. The Please-U cafe had a "Gone" sign. So did the St. Charles Tavern. That was a bad omen because the $8.95 steaks-and-full-bar tavern never closed. Tubby had hoped to buy a belt there. Maybe walking was a bad idea. His stomach growled.

But Igors, "Free Red Beans on Mondays," was open. Only it was Sunday.

He saddled up to the bar and dropped his green bag on the floor. The clunk reminded him he was carrying precious ounces of whiskey and a .45. Igors was a dark and smoky place, but a little less in each category because the double-wide French doors were open to the street.

A seedy-looking guy—Tubby thought he might be a former federal prosecutor—was nursing a Budweiser.

"How's it going?" Tubby inquired politely, looking for the barmaid.

"Magnificent," the man burped. "Absolutely magnificent."

Further inside he could see some fellows playing pool. There was also a washing machine flopping clothes around behind a sudsy window. Beyond that the bar became too obscure to see what was going on.

4

ONNER RIVETTE RODE INTO NEW ORLEANS ON A GREY-
hound from Port Allen with a short stop in Baton Rouge.
When he boarded the bus, the driver mentioned that this
would be the last trip of the day. Everything else into New Orleans
was cancelled for the duration of Hurricane Katrina. That was
fine with Bonner. Just so long as he got there.

He thought the driver looked at him funny, but what the hell.
Everybody else on the bus was stranger than he was. The students
talking in a foreign language wore black pantaloons and had
tattoos on their wrists. The lady with the baby behind him had
eyes popping out of her sockets like a smoked mullet. The fat boy
across the aisle took surreptitious drinks from a green medicine
bottle and wagged his tongue at Bonner after each swallow. Pretty
much the same sort of folks he had endured for two months and
three days in the Pointe Croupee Parish pigsty jail.

"There's a hurricane coming to New Orleans, folks," the driver
lectured them from the front of the bus. "For those of you going through to Hattiesburg, Meridian, Birmingham, and points
north to Atlanta, our layover will not be the forty minutes as
scheduled. Instead of that, we are dropping off our New Orleans
passengers and then getting right back on the road. You will have

just enough time to use the rest rooms, if you like, and stretch your legs. We're only gonna be there about ten minutes, max, so stick close to the bus. This will probably be the last bus into or out of New Orleans."

Bonner got comfortable in his seat. He liked the excitement in the air. The spirits were alive. Here we go, he thought and winked at the passenger across the aisle with the wiggling tongue.

He just stared out the window, watching the trees go by, all the way to New Orleans. The bus got off the Interstate at Gonzales and grabbed Highway 61 south. The driver told them that he was taking the old road because the eastbound lanes of the Interstate were closed by the State Patrol all the way into the city. Everything going toward New Orleans had to take Airline Highway.

The bus made good time, considering the circumstances. It raced past crab shacks, trailer lots, signs for swamp tours and decrepit strip shopping centers, while the oncoming lanes, those heading out of New Orleans, were stalled with too many cars. The bus driver had a radio which he used constantly, speaking into a mike, getting traffic updates. Bonner heard him say that everybody who got on the bus was accounted for.

Once in the city proper, the streets were all virtually empty, and the bus rolled down Tulane Avenue and straight into the terminal. Bonner was in the middle of the crowd getting off. He didn't have any luggage so he shuffled along with the other pilgrims arriving at the cavernous station built for trains. He stopped for a second, pretending to gaze at the wall murals, while he got his bearings and checked for exits. He ran his eyes over the people waiting on the benches and then focused on two men coming toward him. One got right in his face and held up a badge.

"New Orleans Police! You're under arrest, dude," the man said.

His partner crouched, holding a pistol in two hands which

he pointed at Bonner's face. "Hit the floor, sucker!" he commanded.

Bonner licked his lips and spun around. He bolted toward an exit sign, in a direction that put the man with the badge between Bonner and the gun. He might have made it but for an old codger in a wheelchair who was traveling fast across the floor chasing after a wayward toddler. A second's detour was all it took for Detective Johnny Vodka to make the tackle and officer Daneel to slam his gun into Bonner's forehead.

"You're busted, asshole," Vodka breathed into his ear, twisting Rivette's arms around and clamping on the cuffs. "Score another one for the good guys."

While a dribble of blood caked in the cracks above his right eye, Rivette cursed the cops. They on the other hand joked during the whole ride in the squad car to the Parish Prison that it was just like a dumb bum escapee to grab a Greyhound bus, when his description was all over the state. Just like a stupid recidivist to come to New Orleans where he had lived and been arrested twice before.

"Isn't that right, excrement for brains?" Vodka laughed. "Weren't you busted here for assault? See you in court in six months. Or maybe I don't have to go to court for you. Maybe they'll send you straight back to Angola." The cops were happy because they had made a collar of an escaped felon, and no one had gotten hurt in the process.

They took Bonner to Central Lockup and turned him over to the Orleans Parish Criminal Sheriff's Department.

Tubby didn't stay long at Igors. His longest conversation was with the former prosecutor who insisted he had been good at his job because he looked the other way at minor offenses where the accused could make a contribution to the community or was represented by one of the DA's trusted friends. "Today, nobody's got any 'discretion,'" he said, taking care to get the word past his thick tongue. "Just like robots. No 'discretion' at all."

Tubby discreetly departed. He greeted the dusk with bravado. He was only about twenty-five blocks from home.

It was late afternoon now, about five o'clock if his watch could be believed. He had reset it so many times crossing time zones it wasn't always right. The wind was blowing steadily now. A big storm was definitely on the way. Anybody could feel that now. Hurricane weather felt good.

He followed the streetcar tracks running down the grassy middle of St. Charles Avenue. The branches of the crape myrtles on the neutral ground and the live oaks on the sidewalk side swung wildly away from each sudden gust. When the tempo slackened again they waved gently to and fro, waltzing to a tune only they could hear.

Other than the trees there wasn't much action on the street. It was really far too quiet. Tubby noticed that he could hear his own breathing, audible from the exertion of trucking along block after block. There weren't any cars. He began to hum, and then to sing softly. He saw some young kids, hooded sweatshirts over their heads, running down the block. He felt relieved when they darted down a side street. He passed the K&B—sorry, Rite Aid—at Louisiana Avenue. It was locked down tight. A couple of men were drinking beer in liter bottles hidden by brown paper bags in the parking lot. Tubby gave them a loud "Good evening." They nodded back.

It was hard to get reacquainted with one's town when there was no one was around. In fact, New Orleans seemed forlorn and lonesome. Tubby considered slipping a nip from his bag, but a police car, lights atwirl and flashing, came slowly down the Avenue from the direction of the park.

"Mandatory Evacuation!" bleated from the car. Tubby saw a female officer behind the wheel. He smiled and waved as if he understood the rule and knew exactly what he was doing, which he didn't. "Mandatory Evacuation!" the car repeated. Tubby and the messenger continued in opposite directions.

He had hoped to find Fat Harry's open, a good place to buy a beer and a burger and maybe pick up another bottle for the house. But the bar was all shuttered up. He could hear music inside, so he beat on the doors. A bearded gentlemen holding a mop cracked open the massive castle-like gates.

"Are you closed?" Tubby knew it was a dumb question.

The man nodded his head and chewed his mustache.

"How about a hamburger? I'll pay ten bucks."

The man shook his head.

"How about a bottle of Jack? I'll pay twenty bucks."

The man's eyes crossed. He closed the door. Tubby waited hopefully for a few minutes, then gave it up.

A trash can went rolling down the street. A light rain began to fall, blowing around in swirls. The pedestrian realized it was time to get himself under cover.

Down at Central Lockup, Bonner Rivette was scoping around for an escape plan. That would be the only way he'd ever get out of this joint. They had him again, but they didn't appreciate what they had.

He asked one of the few guards when he would be arraigned, "You know, booked?" He thought maybe the man with his slick bald head and polyester black uniform might not speak English. Finally the guard looked him over and said, "Screw your arraignment. There ain't no judges." That was that.

Bonner was in a cell with eight other men, two whites and six blacks. There were no chairs or benches in the cell, so they sat on the floor or leaned against the wall. Bonner squatted next to one of the white guys, who had long shaggy hair and a face toasted by booze or weather to a radiant shade of purple.

"What's the deal with food around here?" he asked. "They gonna feed us?"

"Doesn't look that way," the man grunted. "Say the kitchen's closed. They ain't even got a damn telephone that works." He gestured to the pay phone bolted to the wall. The steel cable dangled uselessly from the box; there was no handset at the end. "Say there's nobody around to fix it. Everybody left town. Can't even call a damn lawyer."

The man displayed a worn business card in his grimy fingers, Bonner saw the name "Dubonnet & Associates."

"Is that a good lawyer?" Bonner asked.

"Oh, hell if I know. It's just something they pass around in here." He flicked the card onto the concrete floor and closed his eyes. Bonner stretched over to get it. "Tubby Dubonnet," he read. He noted the address and stuck the card into his shirt pocket.

He heard two guards talking outside the cell and went to the bars to get their attention. "Yo, officer," he called.

They ignored him.

"Yo, officer," he repeated, and one came over to the bars.

"Are we gonna, like, get a hearing, or have bail set, or get a lawyer or anything?"

"Beats me, fella," the guard said. "I'm leaving here in five minutes to go home and protect my family from assholes like you."

5

T UBBY GOT VERY LITTLE SLEEP THAT SUNDAY NIGHT. FOR a while his television worked just fine, and he could see the ominous approach of Katrina, hour after hour after hour. Just sitting in his kitchen he could see how he was a target. This thing was coming after him personally. And the same message was blaring out of his living room and bedroom. Wherever he went in the house there was a TV. Different channels, but same picture. And he was in the middle of it. It made the adrenaline flow.

Tubby could hear the wind picking up outside, feel the branches of the trees scraping his roof, hear the slamming of loose shutters and shed doors, and the rusty whine of attic ventilators gone crazy. His nerves were winding up. Rain began to come down in loud waves that beat against the sliding glass doors facing the backyard of his house. He tried to make a supper of a can of turtle soup found in the cupboard, but it didn't satisfy. He finished off his bourbon. The Fritos were history. He looked hungrily at his last can of medium black olives. And the storm was still hours away from land.

He ventured outside from time to time, to gauge the torrent, test his stamina against nature, see what odds and ends were blowing up the street, but each time he retreated quickly back to shelter. Wandering through the house he allowed himself some rare introspective moments, not something he typically indulged. A quick inventory of his life produced some good points, like getting married, raising kids, winning the Hambuckle case, settling Darryl Alvarez, meeting Faye Sylvester, not all so bad. His mind blew past the bad parts, like the end of his partnership with Reggie Turntide, like . . . He had to stare for a long moment at his hands to see if there was any blood there. He opened a last bottle of red wine. There wasn't any more booze in the house. He made himself a pot of coffee. At least the gas stove was still working. He tried to call his daughters, but all the phones in the world seemed to be ringing busy.

About midnight the hurricane finally rocked in. Tubby no longer had to watch weather jockeys get blown down the street on his several television sets, now he could hear the wind howl like a jet plane taxiing past his front door and feel his whole house shake. It was deafening and frightening. Burglar alarms went off in houses down the street. Trees snapped and crashed into his home. The floor vibrated. Windows rattled and waves of horizontal rain banged against the few inches of wall that separates any of us from the next life. His neighbor's big hackberry, must have been forty feet tall, came down and loudly crunched the wooden fence between the houses. The ground, the heart-of-pine floor beneath Tubby's feet, bounced when the tree hit. There was the sound of breaking glass, and Tubby hurried upstairs to find that a window had blown out and a jet of water as from a fire hose was shooting over his washer and dryer. Rain pellets, or were they shards of glass, burned his face, and he had to withdraw. He heard a transformer pop outside. All the lights went out.

He managed to get downstairs, feeling his way to the living room sofa. He sat down there and leaned his head back against a pillow, waiting to see what would happen next.

EVEN THE WALLS of Templeman II Prison seemed to shake. Bonner could feel it through the concrete pressing into his back. He listened to the guards talk excitedly outside the cell. Prisoners in other cell blocks were screaming, demanding information. His own group was straining to stay cool, but time was getting short. One guy rocked back and forth on his haunches and appeared ready to spring, teeth bared. Some kept their heads down, covered by elbows and knees. One man paced the room, and another did standing push-ups against the wall.

A dude with a scar on his cheek got in Rivette's face and called him one ugly honky. Bonner grabbed the big man's ears and screamed in his face, "I ain't a honky! I am Katrina," and he kissed the startled inmate on the lips. The man fell away in terror.

This was a new idea that had just come to Bonner Rivette. He had long identified with the woodland spirits, those who had snuck over from Europe with the white race and found new homes, even in the ravine-etched forests of Louisiana, but he had never felt communion with a salt-water wind from the Gulf of Mexico before. It was an attractive ally, if he could just get close enough to it.

As the other prisoners reasoned-out what they had just seen him do, and shuffled away to their separate corners, Bonner settled back to think.

He was starting to get that good feeling again, when his engines ignited and he could smell the arrival of chaos. Bonner had frequently benefited from chaos. It was his friend. He liked it so well he frequently tried to create his own.

6

TUBBY STARTED ABRUPTLY AWAKE. HE HAD DOZED OFF ON the couch while tree branches banged against his walls. What aroused him was that the storm's wind had slackened. He looked at his watch. It read 7:39 AM. He stretched to work out a kink in his back and limped off to check the perimeter.

The laundry room upstairs was a soggy mess, with glass and leaves blown all over the room and out into the hall. A half-inch of water pooled on the linoleum floor. Through the bedroom windows that were intact he saw only gray sky where once there had been a curtain of trees. On the ground below he saw that his yard was buried in limbs.

Downstairs, some sheetrock from the bathroom ceiling had fallen and made a mess in the tub.

Grim-faced, he went outside. It was still raining lightly and the wind blew steadily but at a refreshing speed. A great magnolia had been uprooted, depositing a twenty-foot-high tangle of leaves and branches between his front steps and the street. The old friend had taken all the electric lines down with it. Tubby was careful where he placed his feet. Climbing through his yard, he got a better view of his neighborhood. Fallen trees covered the whole street. Any cars that might be parked along the curbs were out of sight. The magnificent branch of a century-old live oak had lodged in the roof of the house across from his. But by and large, the old homes all seemed to be still standing. The rain made everything slick and treacherous, however. He climbed back through the brush, casting invectives at the scratches and scrapes, and got back inside.

He tried the TV just to be sure it wouldn't work. Then he remembered that the clock radio in the downstairs guest bedroom operated on back-up battery power when the electricity was off. He had learned this once when all the fuses blew. He went to get it, impressed with his own ingenious memory.

WWL clear-channel talk radio was on the air, and the news wasn't so bad. Some of the Superdome roof had been ripped off, but the people inside were mostly dry and well-behaved. The worst of the storm was belting the Mississippi coast and moving inland. Entergy reported about two hundred thousand customers might be without power. Many trees had blown down. There were reports of flooding in the Lower Ninth Ward, but that was to be expected. That's why they called it "lower." Katrina had left a heck of a mess, but the city had basically survived the punch.

Tubby felt tired, but brave. He had been right to stick around, and now he had a story he could tell his grandkids. As the sun rose higher he feasted on dry Wheat Chex with Tony Chacherie's sprinkled on top. A little later in the morning he ventured out again and encountered Charlie Schuman, a doctor he knew, walking his goofy Irish setter around the debris on the sidewalk. They exchanged greetings, and Charlie said he had a freezer full of T-bones and venison that would surely go bad soon. He invited Tubby over for a barbecue that evening, and Tubby said I'll be there.

The rain was entirely gone by early afternoon. The weather was balmy, and Tubby was clearing brush out of his back yard. He took a break and turned on the radio again. There were reports of a breach in the levee on the Seventeenth Street Canal. That was a sad thing. It meant some residences in Lakeview would flood. But it was also about ten miles from Tubby's house.

A while later, a caller on Spud McConnell's talk show was heard to say, "Dude, there's water coming down Carrollton Avenue."

McConnell said, "We cannot confirm what you've just told us."

"Well, man, I'm looking right at it," the caller insisted.

It was the cocktail hour. Tubby wandered outside hoping to find somebody who would offer him one, and he found water rippling over his shoes. It gurgled around among the leaves and branches underfoot. He tried to locate the source by climbing through the brush to the next block, but the water was flowing everywhere and was now ankle-deep. He hacked back to his house thinking he must block the spaces under the doors with towels and get the tools off the floor of his shed.

The freshet was making his yard squishy. It had never been this high before, never. Thoughts of free barbecue were forgotten.

7

FTER HOURS OF DRAGGING EVERYTHING HE CONSIDERED important upstairs, and watching the water rise over his front steps and wash aside his futile barriers, watching it turn his carpets a deeper blue, Tubby fell exhausted onto his bed. He had eaten nothing more than crackers and canned tuna fish for a long time. What day it was no longer mattered. His available fluids now consisted of some brown stuff coming out of the tap, dozens of bottles of Schweppes tonic water and Canada Dry club soda, some very old liquors with dangerous-looking sugar crusted around the caps, and six tiny cans of pineapple juice. He couldn't shave or brush his teeth. He was wary of using the toilet, wondering if the drain might back up into his house, and he was too mad at the whole world to do anything but collapse.

Early Tuesday morning he awoke to a watery wonderland. His sofa bobbed pleasantly in the dining room below. Chairs floated on their backs around the kitchen, taking a much needed rest. He thought of his hip waders, but they were in the garage. He put on old pants, old sneakers, and a scowl and took the final steps down the stairs. The brown tide caught him right below the knees. Trailing a frothy wake, he sloshed to the front door. It was hard to open, but he got it done. The lake was there to meet him. As far as the eye could see. Well, what to do?

Salvaging his boat might be a good idea. He contemplated trying to swim across the yard, but the thought of splashing this stuff into his mouth made his skin crawl. So he went in feet first, and shivered when he sank below his belt before hitting turf. Oh, Lord. Fifty feet to the driveway had never seemed so far. He howled in pain as he turned his ankle in an underwater tree branch.

Then it came over him, the mean jaw, the determination, the will to survive, and he splashed, and stumbled, and forced himself through the awful soup to the *Lost Lady*, his twenty-foot Triton with the Mercury engine. It was still hooked to the trailer and was barely afloat with a foot of rain water inside. Gamely he set to work unstrapping the trailer and bailing out his precious little vessel with a child's red beach bucket that happened merrily along.

PANDEMONIUM REIGNED in the capital of Hell. It was the new Sheriff Mulé's prison located at the bottom of the New Orleans bowl. When the water poured in all the guards ran upstairs. An intrepid captain rallied his men, realizing that common decency required doing something for the hundreds of prisoners chest-deep in the foaming brine. Official communications had all been knocked out. The electricity that powered not just the lights but also the cell locking mechanisms was gone. The office staff had all clocked out the day before. The stranded night shift was entirely on its own.

Bonner was trying to fend off the other lunatics he was stuck with. The man who had been rocking now howled like a blue tick hound baying at the moon. Three or four others had gotten into a shoving match and were thrashing about in the water trying to drown each other. A man pleaded on his knees for the help of the Lord, the fetid water baptizing his shoulders.

Apparently there was not a well-thought-out evacuation plan for this joint.

A few of the black uniforms returned, and they were brave men. They earned twelve thousand dollars a year, and they had families in danger somewhere. Still they were willing to venture into the swill and rescue the cats they were charged with keeping off the streets. They opened up the cell door with some sort of a master key. It took two of them to force the gate across Rivette's cell to slide back.

"Out! Out!" the deputies ordered, pointing to a stairwell at the end of a long corridor. Other prisoners were already swimming in that direction. "Everyone upstairs!" they shouted.

Bonner was one of the last to tread water into the hall. Always the good Samaritan, he dragged behind him the floating corpse of one poor Mexican who had been drowned in the fight.

"Leave that one here!" the guard shouted, and hurried as best he could through the rising water to the front of the line. Bonner saw a door marked ATTORNEY VISITS, PREPARE TO BE SEARCHED, in the opposite direction. He slid down into the water with his corpse and gently drifted away. The door to the visitation room wasn't locked. He left his cellmate behind, and floated on through.

Bonner kept floating, on his back mostly, past a row of visitors' chairs and into the waiting area for the jail. He dog-paddled quietly past the desk where guards would typically be watching everything on their closed-circuit TVs. He reached the front glass door, which unfortunately was locked. No matter. He located a steel chair and smashed through the glass, standing with water up to his armpits. There was no one around to stop him.

Swimming through the glass he found himself in an outdoor walkway within the prison grounds. He still had the perimeter wall to contend with—ten feet of concrete blocks with a New England granite facade topped by a springy coil of razor wire.

Bonner respected that product. He had earned thirty stitches trying to get across it once in Arkansas.

At the risk of recapture, he retraced his route back into the jail and through the attorney visiting area. His Mexican was floating just a few feet from where he'd been left, face down against a Coke machine. Bonner grabbed him by the collar and pulled him along until they were both outside again. A floodlight and generator assembly had been overcome by the deluge, and the light pole had toppled against the wall. Rivette used this as a ladder. He got one arm over the top of the bricks, barely sliding it under the deadly stainless steel knifelets. With all of his strength he pulled his Mexican up and over the coil. The criminal jammed the corpse firmly into the steel teeth so that it would not easily dislodge. The necessary padding was now in place. Taking his time, he worked his own body, inch by inch, out of the water and on top of his new friend. They lay together, while Rivette gasped and spat out sludge, conjugally joined. When Bonner had caught his breath he pushed off and cleared the wire, falling into the water on the other side and leaving his companion stuck behind. He was free once more.

Free, that is, in murky water up to his neck. It was still nighttime, and the city was blacked out. A lake stretched in front of him for hundreds of yards. He did not know it, but he was straining to see across Interstate 10, which was totally engulfed. All he knew was that it looked like a long and dangerous swim to the other side. Rivette summoned the aid of friendly salamanders and snakes. Then he noticed that to his left, just a block away, was an overpass. He could even see dark figures moving about there. Behind him were prison walls and the faint cries of suffering humanity. He started swimming, stroking at an easy pace, toward that overpass.

Tubby got the *Lost Lady* seaworthy. Using a paddle to push past mailboxes and cars, and using the trolling motor sparingly, he managed to proceed onto State Street and over to Claiborne Avenue, where the water was deeper and the sailing smoother. A woman waved at him from the upstairs window of a yellow stucco house, and he carefully puttered in her direction.

"Can you help us?" she pleaded.

"I'll try." He steered into her yard and encountered a submerged hedge. "Far as I can go," he yelled. "Do you think you can swim over here?"

She did, along with a sullen teenager with a tie-dyed shirt and a nose ring, and a little boy about ten who was enjoying the entire adventure. Mom looked tired. Tubby helped them all crawl into the boat.

"Where do you think we should go?" he asked when they were settled in their seats. He was totally inexperienced in nautical rescues on urban streets.

"I don't know," the woman said, irritated, shaking her hair. "Don't you live around here?"

"Yeah, over by State Street. I think I've seen you at Winn-Dixie."

"Mary Jane, quit sucking your hair," the woman scolded. "No telling what awful stuff's in this water. You've rescued us," she told Tubby. "Take us where it's dry."

"Maybe Baptist Hospital would be worth a try," he suggested, not sure he liked this predicament.

"That sounds like a winner," she said, angry at her fate.

Her rescuer backed the boat out of the boxwoods and into the street. He pointed it toward Napoleon Avenue.

"Lordy, there's Mr. Melancon," the woman exclaimed. A man in a checked bathrobe sat atop his roof. Tubby steered that way.

Mr. Melancon had gone up on an aluminum ladder, and he

came down the same way, stopping at the water line and waving for the boat to come in closer. He was wearing wet bedroom slippers over wet white socks, and he had not recently shaved. Tubby brought the boat in close, and the old man stepped in and stumbled into the arms of the teenager, who yelped. The boat rocked, and everybody made noises.

"This is all so stupid," Mr. Melancon griped.

Tubby finally got them positioned. "Off we go again."

On the way to Napoleon Avenue they passed other stranded people, but five was about all the *Lost Lady* was rated to carry so Tubby just kept going. He made a tight turn toward the river and Baptist Hospital, still unsure of his depth. They got to the Emergency Entrance but the hospital was in water well up to the first floor and was as deserted as could be.

"I suppose they got all the patients out," the mother said.

Suddenly there was the sound of breaking glass and a chair sailed through a window six flights up.

A head poked out.

"Send help!" the person cried. "It's very hot in here!"

"Mom, look, what's that?" the kid asked, looking into the water.

Tubby followed the pointing finger and saw what appeared to be toes and a nose floating toward them. He gunned his little trawler and hastened away. "The highest ground will be at the levee," he said sagely.

He was right, but he didn't have to go all the way to the levee to prove it. Just a few blocks further on, right by one of Tubby's favorite eateries, Pascal's Manale, the *Lost Lady* scraped pavement.

"I guess you'll have to walk from here," he told his passengers. "I think I can see dry land ahead at St. Charles Avenue."

"Maybe we can catch a streetcar," the lady said bitterly. She got her family and Mr. Melancon over the side into water only about a foot deep. There were blue flashing lights at St. Charles, the signals emitted by welcoming police cars. "Are you coming?" she asked Tubby.

"No, I'm going back," he told her. Keep your daughter and Mr. Melancon, too. "If those guys are cops, tell them there are people who need help at the hospital."

He waited until his refugees had splashed out of the flood, and then he used his paddle to shove off. The *Lost Lady* took him back the way they had come, up Napoleon Avenue. His plan was to make at least one more trip bringing in survivors, ferrying people to solid ground. When he got back to the intersection at Claiborne, however, he saw a gleeful group of wet young men using a street sign to break in the door of the Walgreen's. He reached into his green bag for his firearm, checked it for water, and placed in on his lap. Tubby was not a believer in guns. He had devoted more than two decades to the law. The speed with which he was now reverting to self-protection surprised even him.

A few minutes later, as he neared his own neighborhood, another boat, a flat-bottomed pirogue better suited for duck hunting in marsh grass, came wobbly out of Cuculu Street manned by two young studs, and it steered right at Tubby.

He opened up the throttle on his motor, but even one enthusiastic paddler could beat him, and the pirogue angled to cut him off.

The boy in front displayed a weapon with a black barrel and a plastic stock that could have been an AK-47 for all Tubby knew. The lawyer showed off his own handgun, pointing it at the sky. The boy on the back seat stopped paddling, and the two boats passed each other, stern looks all around. No words were spoken though Tubby had a few he felt like saying.

He kept an eye on the pirogue as it receded into the distance and cut left onto a side street. They wanted my boat, he thought to himself. He felt a branch scrape the hull. "Heading home," he said out loud and made a bee-line for his soggy hearth.

That night found Tubby mixing up strange concoctions. Always a fan of inventive New Orleans cuisine, he first tried, then rejected, cold canned mushroom soup mixed with club soda. Inspired by a can of artichoke hearts, he took his time and made a remoulade sauce. He mixed the horseradish from the jar with the mustard and paprika and salad oil, Worstershire sauce, and Crystal hot sauce, and a little vinegar, the black pepper, the white pepper, and he had it. He poured this over his artichokes and ate with satisfaction.

Later, he sat on his upstairs balcony in a rocking chair, trying to sleep while mosquitoes buzzed, cradling his .45 on his lap. Clouds were finally giving way to stars, whole constellations of them. He could see the muses. The City of New Orleans was that dark.

8

BONNER THE CRIMINAL WAS AS HAPPY AS A KID WITH AN ice cream cone when he reached the Broad Street overpass and dragged himself out of the water. First off, there were helpless women and children on the bridge, huddled around small fires and swatting bugs. The couple of men he saw looked old and weak, and they also had clothes that might fit him. Even ragged jeans would serve him better than the orange prison jumpsuit he had on. Anyone with a brain could figure out where he got that. Best of all, there were no cops in sight.

"Howdy ma'am," he said to one old crone bent over a trash fire with two mournful looking kids sitting beside her.

"Howdy yourself. You got anything to eat?"

"No, I don't," Bonner admitted.

"Here's something if you want it." She poked a granola bar in Bonner's face, and he accepted it gratefully.

"Guess I'll look around," he said and stood up.

"Ain't much to see," she told him.

He walked to the top of the bridge, which spanned Lake Interstate, and down the other side where the roadway sank beneath the flood. Just ahead, though Bonner couldn't have identified it, was the Melpomene Street Pumping Station No. 1. It was silent as a tomb, its 2.6 million gallon per minute screws under water and powered off for the duration. Bonner noted several other campers. There were about twenty all told, he figured. Nobody was overtly friendly or curious. It was dark. Everybody was wet and miserable. Bonner found a spot by himself and lay down, his back propped against the concrete guard rail. His sleep, occasionally interrupted by helicopters flapping overhead, was fitful.

He woke up hungry. The sun was coming up over the parish prison, and the silhouetted guard towers reminded him of the urgency of travel. The other bridge-dwellers were stirring about. Of course they would notice his clothes, and somebody might have the bravado to say something about it. He wondered which way to go. He watched two kids swim toward him to the overpass. They got out dripping, clutching plastic bags, and walked among the groups of refugees offering cans of Vienna sausages and bags of chips for sale. Bonner shook his head angrily and waved them off. If they could find food, so could he.

He was preparing to dive in himself when he saw he had waited too long. A boat with two SWAT-team officers tied off at one end of the bridge. As soon as he saw them, Bonner walked the other way quickly. There was a female sleeping beside the crone, the one who had given him the granola bar. The prone figure clutched a worn poncho around her shoulders. He poked her once in the ribs and pulled the poncho off her back.

"Hey, what—" She sat up. The old lady started to say something. Bonner put one finger to her lips, "SHHH," and wrapped the blanket over himself to hide his uniform. He could not see the officers now. The woman he had ripped the cover from was too weak to protest, and she lay back down.

Then it got worse. Two white buses had been parked in front of the prison, water over their tires. They began to move, creating a wide wake, driving slowly toward the overpass. Miraculously, they navigated the hundred yards belching exhaust bubbles and crept triumphantly onto the pavement. They chugged to the top of the overpass and stopped. A pair of prison guards got out and had a conference. They had brought with them about forty inmates each. Through the wrinkles of his poncho Bonner saw the SWAT guys again. They hiked up their side of the ramp and huddled with the guards. Bonner looked up at the windows of the buses. He saw lots of faces. Surely the prisoners inside could see him and imagine who he was. He stayed as still as possible. The old woman beside him also watched in silence. The day went on.

Many more refugees arrived on the Broad Street overpass on Wednesday. They swam in or came by boat. The SWAT guys finally left for someplace else. A food vendor showed up in front of Bonner and offered a can of Lay's Bean Dip for five dollars. Bonner grabbed the man by the throat and whacked his head into the concrete abutment. He tossed the can of dip to the old lady. He muscled the scalper over behind one of the white prison buses. "Meet Katrina, buddy," he whispered in the unconscious man's ear. Bonner liked the sound of his new voice. Glancing quickly up at the rear window of the bus, he saw eyes disappear. He bashed the man's skull on the concrete a couple more times, and then began to undress him. It took only a few minutes to steal a pair of filthy wet blue jeans, an Acme Oyster House T-shirt, and a pair of Adidas. Bonner stripped off his own prison garb and put on the new clothes. He tossed his orange jump-suit over the side. Then he tossed the food salesman over the side. Then he jumped over the side and began paddling downtown.

AT THE PLACE PALAIS, alone with an empty building to protect, Manuel the security guard had lots of time to reflect about what is truly important in life. In normal times his wife and kids drove him crazy. When he was at home he couldn't even read the newspaper at night or watch his favorite shows for all the interference. It had been so long since he'd had the TV to himself, his shows probably weren't even on anymore. He couldn't take off his shoes without hearing that his feet smelled. He couldn't yell at his son without his wife sticking up for the kid. She crabbed all the time, and wasn't interested in sex. Then she bitched at him for always being angry and going to bed early. So, normally, he liked being at work.

But now he missed the whole crew of them. Manuel had not seen his family for two days, and he did not know where they were. On the police band at his security office, he learned that Chalmette, the town where he lived, was flooded. His house was near the Forty Arpent Canal which would be the most dangerous place to be if the levee broke.

No one from building management had called or shown up. The land-lines were still working, but he couldn't connect with anyone. He had tried to reach Bucky, the chief of operations, but just got his voice mail. When he called Bucky's home phone the line rang busy.

It was an important job, being in charge of a forty-nine-story office building, but what the hell. All he could see on his security cameras were grainy black-and-white images of empty floor after empty floor. The cameras focused on the loading bays and the front doors revealed lots of water in the streets and very little else. Sometimes a person waded or floated by. The battery was running out on the cameras anyway.

The lights in Manuel's office and one elevator worked only because he kept feeding gas to the emergency generator. He had enough for about twelve more hours, but did he want to stay here that long?

A week ago they had been planning their vacation at the beach—Fort Morgan, Alabama, the redneck Riviera. Hell, this was supposed to be his vacation time. Family, that's what's important in life. If you ain't got family, what have you got? You've got a job, with thirteen years built towards retirement, and a 401k. You can't just leave. What if someone broke in? And did what? Loot the shops on the first floor? And how am I supposed to stop them? With one handgun and a case of pepper spray? Should I call 911? Manuel laughed to himself. It was a bitter laugh. Where's Bucky, I wonder? Baton Rouge, at a Holiday Inn, no doubt. (Actually, Bucky was in Providence, Rhode Island, conferring with the company brass about ways to maximize their insurance claim.) The whole damn city may be flooded, and I'm here alone. Where are the soldiers? Why am I the one stuck?

Manuel looked at his half-eaten Payday candy bar, wrapper folded back, peanut crumbs escaping, on his desk.

"I'm getting hungry. And I am sick and tired of eating candy," he said to the walls.

BONNER PADDLED from Broad Street all the way downtown to the main public library. At that point he could stand up and wade. Along the way he had hidden from police boats, run into trash cans lurking beneath the water, made a circle around swimming rats, avoided dogs baying from rooftops, watched old people dangling from windows, seen tons of garbage drifting aimlessly in the current, and witnessed the looting of a liquor store.

He had a destination in mind, though he wasn't sure what he would find there or how permanent it would be. No matter. Bonner survived by being flexible. That was the way of nature, and Bonner had grown up in the woods. His father hardly ever knew where he was, and his mother was a drug whore. That's a fact. Fortunately he had an uncle, an old corn farmer who owned some land down the road and fed him and exposed the young and impressionable Bonner to books. The boy was versed in all the Aryan principles, but he had an independent streak and rejected many of them. For example, he never accepted that the mud people were the enemy. Hell, they sounded just like mom and pop. For a time he was worried about the "Money Changers' Servants," as portrayed by the Little Flower of Jesus. But then he encountered the works of some little-noticed German and West Virginian tract-writers and concluded that all humanity was the enemy. The cops, the teachers, the jails, the parents, and the towns they lived in. But he rejected the Christian part because he didn't see its relevance to the woodland powers. He saw a mission for himself to lead these Teutonic spirits into battle against every ugly element of so-called modern society, and this view was supported by the fact that nobody else his age liked him, and he did not like them either.

The hurricane had revealed to Bonner that there was another vast power he had never expected, and it came from the sea. He had never seen salt water, and he was as curious as any young man would be. Girls with bikinis dwelt there, and they had to be obliterated, too, which was quite confusing to his mind.

Rivette's immediate destination was the law office of Dubonnet & Associates. Number one, he might find a lawyer he could get help from or rip off. Number two, it was the only address he had in New Orleans, except an old house in Harahan where he had briefly lived, and that was too far away. Number three, if he were caught by the police while trying to reach the Place Palais, he had a pretty good excuse. Which was, your Honor, I was not tying to escape, I was washed away by the flood and I was trying to reach my lawyer so he could tell me how to give myself up.

By the time he got into the New Orleans business district he was walking in only a few inches of water and trying to straighten out his funky clothes. He wasn't sure where the Place Palais was. He saw only one police car rolling on the streets, but there were other figures lurking about. He kept to the shadows of buildings and doorways. It was urgent to stay out of sight.

MANUEL HAD HAD IT. He stuck his unfinished Julie Smith mystery and an unopened bottle of water into his red nylon satchel, checked the gun on his waistband, stuffed a handful of keys and access cards into his pocket, and walked down the frozen escalator to the first floor. The lobby, given over to retail shops, was as deserted as a tomb, and his steps echoed off the marble . Stylishly dressed mannequins stared blankly at him from behind their imprisoning windows. He hurried to the tall glass entrance doors and made sure they were locked. Then he descended the service stairs to the freight entrance. He came out on a pitch-black loading platform. Manuel felt his way down a short flight of concrete steps and walked across the empty bay to the emergency exit. He had the master key ready in his hand, but he knew it would not be necessary. This door opened freely from within. He pushed hard and was out in the street. Finally he was free to go about his own business.

Bonner Rivette, still wet, was hiding inside what had once been the doorway of the Bun and Biscuit. Now it was an abscess in the building with a wrecked aluminum frame showered in broken glass. He was standing among the shards when he saw Manuel come out of the emergency door. He saw the glint of the security man's badge. He also saw Manuel take a big ring of keys, try to attach them to a ring on his belt, then stuff them into a red bag. The security man turned left on the sidewalk, which brought him very close to Bonner.

The criminal used a concrete block to put Manuel on the ground. It was that quick. Muttering, "I got you," he pulled the senseless form into the wreckage of the biscuit restaurant and went through the man's pouch and hip pockets. The guy was still breathing, so Rivette used the guard's own handcuffs and locked him to a standpipe. He collected the keys, a batch of access cards, a can of Mace, and a small handgun. He scurried to the building's back entrance and tried keys in the door until he found one that fit. He jumped inside and pulled the door shut behind him.

Bonner Rivette became the sole watchman over Place Palais. It was his own lightless castle.

"This isn't bad at all," he thought when he emerged from the loading dock into the world of retail. A bank branch, a dress shop, luggage, shoes, the whole enchilada. He tried the master key on a men's clothing store and it worked. He waited for the alarm to sound. When he heard nothing, and saw no blinking red lights, he went for a quick shopping spree. What he came up with, groping in the dark, was a blue sports shirt with a nautical emblem on its chest. This was a valuable addition and a step-up from the T-shirt he had swiped from the looter on the bridge. A belt, a couple of pairs of socks, and a pack of underwear and he was good to go. He ran a circle around the fountain that was the centerpiece of the mall. There was a statue there of a Mediterranean goddess smiling down on him. He pumped his fists in tribute.

Realizing that he was spending a lot of time in a public place and that there might be other dwellers in this concrete realm, Rivette went exploring. He found a directory mounted on a marble podium behind a glass plate, which he perceived as the layout of the enemy's compound. By putting his eyes close to the glass he could confirm that Dubonnet & Associates was still where the card had said, in Suite 4300, meaning floor forty-three. He had some knowledge of how cities worked since he had once been a janitor.

Rivette chanced upon the security desk. He found a half-eaten Payday candy bar and several packs of cheese crackers which he devoured on the spot. He washed them down with a bottle of

Fiji water. He tried the elevators, mashing buttons till he found one that worked.

When he reached the lawyer's office he could see the name on the door, backlit by a red EXIT sign. There was no hole for his master key, but he worked the security man's cards in a slot until one did the job. Inside, the office was as empty as he had hoped. It was black as ink and as remote from sight as any escapee could wish. Now he could rest. He walked the carpeted hall stealthily, poking his nose into each dark room. It felt secure. He returned to the reception area and lay down on its leather sofa. Within minutes he was out, enjoying his first good sleep in five days.

9

Tubby Dubonnet jerked awake more than once during the second night after the storm. One event was the sound of glass shattering somewhere nearby. That kept him on edge for half an hour, straining to see in the darkness, weapon at ready, but the silence put him back down again. Another time he imagined faint screaming. He stood up to peer anxiously over the porch rail. The night was hot and breezy. For fear that his plumbing did not work, he urinated off the porch into the pond of his yard below. He inhaled the earthy, mushroom smell of lake water seeping into places it was not supposed to be, extracting the cleanser from inside kitchen cabinets, the grease from car chassis, the fluff from baby's blankets, the mysterious sandy granules from within sheetrock walls, the gasoline from lawn mowers, the tannin from heaps of twigs and piles of leaves, the dyes of Oriental rugs, the garbage from black plastic bags formerly in cans. He drifted back to sleep.

Dawn came and with it a furious sun. Tubby, sweaty, smelly and bummed, decided it was time to find refuge. The water had risen even more overnight, and his trusty *Lost Lady* strained at the line holding her to the front railing. He put his remaining water and the green bag with the change of clothes aboard, and kept his handgun in his pocket. The shotgun he hid in the house, between the mattresses of his bed. He was afraid to brush his teeth in what was coming out of the faucets, so he squirted some toothpaste into his mouth and ate it.

Ho, Ho, ho and a bottle of rum, he thought as he got back into the boat. Only there is no more rum, and that was another problem. He trolled back to Claiborne, more familiar now with the underwater obstacles. As he turned downtown he saw another boat coming toward him under what seemed to a dangerous amount of power.

Tubby, now a survivalist, readied his pistol again, but as the other vessel drew near he saw that it was occupied by two men wearing T-shirts with POLICE written on them. He put the motor in neutral and waited for the other craft to heave to.

The officer up front, a dark-skinned man with muscles bulging, asked, "Do you live around here?"

Tubby explained who he was.

"We need your boat," the policeman told him. "There are a lot of people stranded in their houses."

"Okay, I guess, but what about me?" Tubby asked.

"I'll put Officer Jones with you, and you can drive, if you're willing to help rescue people."

Tubby was willing, and after some maneuvering they got Officer Jones into the *Lost Lady*. He plunked down behind Tubby.

"You know the neighborhood?" the captain of the other boat asked.

"Sure. I've lived here for years."

"Then you can take her up the side streets on that side of Claiborne," he pointed toward the lake, "and I'll go on this side of Claiborne. Anybody you can rescue goes down to the Superdome."

"Right," Tubby said. "You got any food?"

"Here's some water. There should be food at the Superdome." He tossed one bottle, then another, into the air, and Officer Jones caught them. The policeman opened one for himself and handed the other to his oarsman.

"Later," the flood warrior said, and shot away.

"I guess we can look around Jefferson Avenue," Tubby suggested.

"My house is by the Rendon Inn," Officer Jones said.

"You want to go by your house?"

"Yeah, let's go there first."

"Suits me." Tubby headed to Jefferson Avenue and made his left.

"This is really bad," he said. All the houses in this section were flooded. The water reached half-way up the windows on the first floor. Luggage racks protruded above the surface where SUVs were parked. "What a mess," he said in awe.

Officer Jones just grunted. They didn't see anyone needing rescue, though they spotted a couple of rafts in the distance when they crossed Fountainbleu.

"They may be looters," Tubby suggested.

Officer Jones just grunted again. A palm tree felled across the street was creating a dam and a small waterfall. Tubby edged through a lawn to get onto Jefferson Davis Parkway. Everything here was wrecked.

"These were nice homes," Tubby said aloud, talking to himself since Officer Jones didn't seem to want to communicate. There was a man in a second floor window, and Tubby waved at him. The man gestured with a rifle, and Tubby waved good-bye.

"Rendon Inn, coming up."

"I live on Eden, up on the right," Jones informed him.

"Tell me when."

"When," Officer Jones said after they had gone another block.

Tubby throttled back. Officer Jones stared at the roof of a brick ranch-style house. "Get me over there," he ordered.

Tubby steered the *Lost Lady* to the roof, worried about hidden vehicles, bird baths, and telephone lines

Officer Jones leapt to the asphalt shingles while Tubby tried to keep the boat from capsizing. Like a crab he ascended to the top of the dry roof and grasped the bright, silver attic ventilator. Giving it a bear hug and emitting a howl he twisted it off and threw it aside. Tubby saw him stick his head into the hole, then come back up.

"You got an axe?" Jones bellowed.

Tubby shook his head, no. He watched the officer begin kicking the roof with his heavy boots. Kicking and kicking until he had the hole big enough so that he could lie flat on the black shingles and put his shoulders through. Tubby tried to find a place to tie the boat off so he could help, but the roof sloped down beneath the water. Before he could sort out the problem Officer Jones had extracted a baby wearing blue pajamas. He scooted down the roof and handed the infant to Tubby, who tried very hard not to drop it while rocking back and forth. The policeman went up again and began cajoling, almost in a sing-song, and ultimately bringing a squirming woman out of the hole. She was wearing a flowery nightgown over a pair of ripped blue jeans. She planted herself on the crown of the roof, and Jones tried to get her to stand up. The woman was having nothing of that. Arms crossed tightly over her breasts, she prayed loudly but allowed herself to be pulled in a sitting position down the roof to the boat. At a loss, Tubby secured the baby in his ice chest and lent a hand to get the woman get on board. Officer Jones almost tilted them over when he jumped in. Tubby sat the woman down, and Jones put his arms around her. The ice chest with the baby was right behind them. The kid stuck its head up and cried.

"Go! go!" Jones commanded. The policeman was upset. The woman was in shock.

"The Superdome?" Tubby asked.

"Just go, now!"

Tubby got behind the wheel and away they went. As he passed the Blue Plate Mayonnaise factory, he saw an island much closer than the Superdome; it was the Broad Street overpass, and he could see that there were people and buses on the bridge.

It took just a few minutes to get there. The people on the overpass drew back as if afraid when the *Lost Lady* motored up and idled at the edge of the flood. Then, when they saw the POLICE T-shirt, they crowded around.

"Find out if there are any more cops here!" Jones instructed Tubby. He stayed in the boat with his woman and baby. Tubby climbed out, got his land legs back, and worked through the crowd.

"Have you got food?" the people asked. "Where are the helicopters?" "When are they coming for us?" The lawyer just shook his head. He hoped Jones could protect the boat. The buses at the top of the bridge had "Orleans Parish Prison" written on the side. He rapped on the door of the first one, but it was a man sitting on top of the bus with a shotgun on his lap who responded.

"Who are you?" the guard demanded.

"My name is Dubonnet. I'm with the policeman over there in the boat. Are there any cops around? What's going on?"

"No, there ain't no cops around. I've got forty-two prisoners in this bus and forty-four in the other one. You want them?" Some of the guys in the bus started beating on the glass.

"No food!" they yelled. "No water!" The bus started to rock. Tubby stepped back.

"Get us out of here!" the prisoners cried.

A woman grabbed his arm.

"There's a sick one there," the woman said, pulling Tubby toward a heap of clothes lying on the pavement. "I don't know what's wrong with her, but she needs a doctor now."

Tubby looked, and indeed it was a woman, a fairly young one, hair streaked with dirt, eyes closed, sweating. Her legs looked lifeless on the paving, and her head was supported uncomfortably by the curb.

"Is no one helping you here?" he asked.

The old woman shook her head. "Take this one with you before she dies. Please."

Tubby carried the woman off the bridge, parting the crowd as he went. She wasn't light. Her skin was soft but cold. Some of the refugees were too tired to get out of their way, and the lawyer had to step over them. Others cursed him for leaving them behind.

Officer Jones initially looked like he wouldn't let another passenger on board, but Tubby handed him the woman, and he took her anyway. The captain got aboard, regained the wheel, and motored back into the flood.

"We'll go to the Convention Center," Jones stated firmly. "That's where we'll find the buses."

10

BONNER AWOKE ON THE LEATHER SOFA AND TOOK IN HIS new surroundings. A framed Jazz Fest poster, a quiet room. Sunlight came through the windows in the back. He got to his feet and went looking for water. There was a combination kitchen and copy machine room in the law office. Water trickled thinly into the sink, but there was also a Kentwood dispenser with a nearly full five-gallon bottle. He lifted the jug out and washed his face, letting the water splash onto the floor.

A splendid sunrise poured into Tubby's office. Bonner liked it here. He could see all over New Orleans. Toward the west, rooftops poked out of the silvery glittering soup of lake water. Below him the French Quarter appeared to be high and dry. Other office towers were close by. Curtains flapped from blown-out windows in the Sheraton Hotel.

It was very quiet this high up. No sirens or anything.

He went to work snooping around Tubby's desk. There was a framed photograph of three girls. They were cute. Here was a calendar, and on the first page were some handwritten birthdays, for Collette, Christine, and Debbie. That would make Debbie twenty-two. Christine would be nineteen. She must be the middle one on the picture. Debbie was the one he liked the best. In a Rolodex he found everybody's phone number.

How could he play this to his advantage? He took some time with the question while he explored the other offices. He had just about everything one might need except food. It struck him that the best way to get something to eat would be to have somebody bring it to him.

The phone had a dial tone. Bonner cocked his head quizzically as he played with the buttons until he figured out it didn't matter which line he picked. He tried Debbie's number first. It rang once then turned into static. Frowning he looked for the middle child, Christine. She might do. There were two numbers. The first one he tried also produced a busy signal, but the second one rang. It rang and rang, and then a voice message came on.

"Hello, if you would like to leave me a message, wait for the tone."

He hung up. It was a pretty voice, but he wasn't ready to talk into a recording device.

The third number belonged to the youngest. She was barely a teenager. Excited, he tried it but was rewarded with nothing except electronic beeps. He stared angrily at the phone and put it softly back in its cradle.

Bonner hadn't really thought out what he would do after he escaped. He had just reacted to events and opportunities. He stole street clothes when he had the chance. He came to this office building because he had the address and had a hunch he might find it empty, but if the building had been a pile of rubble he would have thought of something else. Bonner's mind was good in that respect.

Mental integrity was important. His sister had gone into high school wild as a bobcat but she had discarded her principles and got religion. She turned proper and bought new clothes and began going to church all the time. When she took up with the preacher, on the sly, they started praying for Bonner's soul, even after he told them to quit it. He knew when they were doing it because their prayers invaded his thoughts. It was nothing but pure betrayal, the way his sister treated him. It boiled over when she and the preacher tried to wrestle him into his sister's station wagon to take him to some holy-roller revival. They would de-Satanize him, they screamed. That scared Bonner. Big mistake. "Satan has nothing to do with me," he shrieked, and in a burst of unplanned violence he carved them up like he was field-dressing a couple of deer.

Rivette figured he could stay in the lawyer's office for at least another day or two without anybody noticing him, considering the degree of social disorder below. But he thought through his other alternatives as well. He remembered the typical mayhem of the French Quarter from his earlier time here, before he had been busted for the senseless charge of attempted rape. He hadn't planned sex. But she slapped him on the jaw and he got mad. He remembered the bars, the girlie joints, the appealing confusion. He also remembered the lack of sympathy for a man without cash, a bum, and that is what he looked like. He could spend some time here in this building getting dressed up. Maybe there was some money around. His stomach growled. The phone rang.

Bonner started at the plastic box on Tubby's desk while it rang three times. Then his hand shot forward and grabbed the phone.

"Hello," he said coughing, disguising his voice.

There was a pause "Did someone call me from this number?" It was a nice girl's voice.

"Is this the lawyer's daughter, Mr. Dew-bonnet?"

"Yes," he heard her almost laugh. "That would be Dew-bone-ay."

Bonner cursed himself for the mistake. He was afraid he might have blown it.

"Sorry, miss. He's had an accident. Are you here in New Orleans?"

"Yes, I'm here," concern in her voice. "What kind of accident? You're calling from Daddy's office, right?"

"He fell on the stairs," Bonner improvised. "How far away do you live?"

"Live? Right now I'm in Fauberg Marigny."

Bonner didn't know where that was.

"Can you come here?" he asked.

"What's wrong with my father? Who are you?"

Bonner was afraid he might have screwed everything up. She knew where he was, but he didn't know where she was or what she might do. Still, this was fun.

"This is Joe, building security. Mr. Dubonnet"—he got it right this time—"slipped and fell on the stairs. He's hurt bad. He probably should go to the hospital, but I don't think there's one open. He told me to call you. Then he passed out."

"Oh goodness," Christine wept.

"So, is it possible for you to get over here and take a look at him?"

"Yes. I'm all by myself, but I can come."

Bonner grinned. "Listen," he said. "I think part of your father's problem may be that he needs food. Could you bring some?"

"Like what?" she was getting hysterical.

"I don't know. Cold cuts, ham. A loaf of bread. Cheese maybe. And hurry if you can."

"I will."

"I'll let you in at the freight entrance beside the building. All the front doors are locked."

"I'll be there as soon as I can."

"You'd better hurry," Bonner said, and he hung up.

Christine was indeed alone. She had decided to stay in New Orleans instead of evacuating with her Tulane classmates. The allure of remaining behind with her boyfriend had been too great, even if they were going to stay at his mother's apartment near the French Quarter. But the mother had started to go nuts after the power went out. She had screamed at both her son and at Christine, accusing them of not understanding that they were all going to die. She wanted to go to Montreal, where her brother lived. Canada was immune to hurricanes. She wanted to go *now!*

Christine and her boyfriend got into a big fight, too, made worse because this was all taking place in a one-bedroom apartment and the mother kept jumping in and adding her own comments. Christine got exasperated and ultimately refused to go anywhere with these people. The mother refused to stay. Christine said she would sleep on the streets and take care of herself. The boyfriend slammed the apartment keys in the dinette and said she should at least stay where it was dry. He drove his mom away in her 2003 Volvo, packed to the roof with her macramé dolls.

So Christine had the place to herself. The street outside was littered with debris but dry. The whole neighborhood, built three hundred years before along the banks of the Mississippi River, had escaped the flood. She had no car, but she did have a bicycle.

Yes, there was a mandatory evacuation, but she had not seen a vehicle or a policeman for at least twenty-four hours. She dragged the bike outside and, cotton blouse flapping in the breeze, she peddled down Chartres Street into the French Quarter headed for the Place Palais. In her school backpack she carried French bread, olives, Brie cheese, a tomato, and a hunk of aging roast beef.

TUBBY GOT HIS MOTOR BOAT, the policeman, the baby-in-the-ice-chest, and two women as far as St. Charles Avenue before he ran aground. They were still about ten blocks short of the Convention Center, but the streets looked friendlier. There was a police car parked where the water stopped. Tubby tied the *Lost Lady* to a traffic light pole.

Officer Jones clambered out and got his comrades' attention, and he and his family got into the squad car and drove away. Tubby got another officer who was pacing around trying to get his phone to work to take a look at the sick woman Tubby had brought along, who was now conscious and sitting up. Some color had returned to her face, possibly as a result of the psychological lift of getting off the bridge. The policeman offered her a bottle of water.

He said if they waited here someone eventually might drive them to the Convention Center where medical attention might be available.

"Can I leave my boat where it is?" Tubby asked.

"We're going to have to requisition that, sir."

"Yes, well it's already been requisitioned. But who should I turn the keys over to?"

"Leave them in the switch. Your boat has been taken by the First District Police." The officer became engaged in conversation with a troupe of muddy hikers who wanted to know where they might find a dry bed.

"Perhaps you could give me some sort of receipt for the boat," Tubby suggested hopefully. The officer ignored him. In truth Tubby felt guilty saying anything about it. After all, this was a national disaster.

He and the woman he had saved sat on the curb. Tubby twisted the cap off his plastic bottle of Evian.

"Name's Tubby Dubonnet," he said

"Hope Lestella," she replied. "Thanks for getting me this far."

She brushed the hair from her forehead. And took a swig of water. Tubby admired the muscles in her throat. She wasn't as old as he had thought, and she might even be pretty when she wiped the mud off her oval face with the prominent chin and big nose. He liked big noses.

Though spared the full brunt of the flood, the block had obviously been struck by a catastrophe. The poles which carried the juice for the streetcars were down on the ground. So was the sign advertising the Great Free Will Mission Pentecostal Apostolic Church, lots of roofing slates, and plenty of trash. The street also smelled.

Two policemen jumped into Tubby's boat. He stood up to say something like, Be careful with her, she's a great . . . but they pushed off into the water and took off before he could make his contribution.

"I guess I'm stuck here," he said to the world.

"I'm stuck, too," Hope Lestella said.

"What was the problem you were having?" Tubby asked her, meaning her health problem.

"Nothing but my house washed away and everything I own is gone. I haven't had a bath or a meal in two days. Or is it three. Other than that . . ."

"Is that why you passed out, is what I mean?"

"Oh, yeah. I'm a diabetic, too. See any Coca-Colas around here?"

Tubby went to look. There was a Sewell Cadillac stretch limousine serving as a sort of community center. But the driver, who looked like a cop, didn't have any sodas. He did have some grape drink powder from an MRE, and Tubby could mix that in a bottle of water, which the cop provided. For Cokes, they recommended the Convention Center and laughed.

Tubby didn't get the joke, but he said thanks and took the

drink back to his new friend. They mixed up the concoction, using the whole flavor packet, and Hope chugged about half of it.

"That's swell," she gasped and made a polite burp.

"You think you could walk a few blocks?" he asked.

"I guess."

"They're telling all of us to go to the Ernest Morial Convention Center. They say there's food there, and it's dry."

"Just as long as it's air conditioned." She got up and dusted her behind.

Tubby took her arm and they embarked on their journey under the Pontchartrain Expressway. Why had the limousine driver laughed?

A young man carrying a desktop computer and another carrying a monitor and keyboard crossed their path, nodded and kept going.

"Maybe they're looting Office Depot," Tubby suggested.

Hope shivered. "The police are just a few feet away."

"Doesn't seem to bother those guys." He tightened his grip on his green bag. Two more youths ran from pillar to pillar under the expressway ahead of them. Tubby worked loose the Velcro flap on the bag and slipped his fingers inside. He found the comfort of the metal grip. The boys laughed and scampered away. A woman sitting in the damp shadow of an overpass pillar surprised them, but she was not aggressive. She was just minding a pile of acquired merchandise, a microwave, a vacuum cleaner, a table lamp.

"This is a dangerous place to be," Tubby whispered.

Boys on battery-powered scooters zipped up the street, hands clutching plastic bags full of booty.

"Let's hurry," Hope suggested.

And they did, as fast as her legs and his dignity would permit. Tubby took out his pistol and carried it by his thigh.

"Hard to believe this is 2005," he said. "Feels like the Wild freakin' West."

The Convention Center was visible, three long empty blocks away.

"I need to rest," Hope sighed, and she sagged onto the sidewalk. "You can go ahead without me."

Tubby hacked out a miserable chuckle. Then he started laughing out loud. Then he was overcome with mirth. He sat down beside his new companion. "Whoo, whee," he exhaled, recovering himself.

"It wasn't that funny," she said. "I'm taking a little nap."

She put her head on Tubby's shoulder, and he rested his head on hers. He had an outdated handgun in his lap, and his rump was getting cold and wet from the pebbly pavement. Displaced urbanites were circling the neighborhood in search of carrion. Bolivia had never looked so sweet. Laughter kept bubbling up. His body shook, but he tried not to disturb his partner. "Now I know what it means," he crooned, "to miss New Orleans."

11

CHRISTINE'S BIKE RIDE THROUGH THE FRENCH QUARTER was a brand new experience. She had never seen the place empty of people. She had never imagined Bourbon Street still, littered not with beer cups but with smashed neon signs and roof slates. Antoine's restaurant seemed to have fallen in on itself. A lost dog ran purposefully down the street, pretending to know where it was going. There were no cops around. It was eerie. She pedaled faster.

Well, a couple of men sat high above the street behind the ornate cast iron rail of a balcony, sipping drinks. That looked normal. And there were some policemen guarding the parking lot under the Marriott Hotel. She pedaled past. Canal Street was empty of cars except those abandoned at the curb. She had to swerve around downed street lamps and streetcar wires, but unless all the glass on the pavement popped her tires she was going through.

She wheeled up to the St. Charles Avenue side of the Place Palais. Since it was the freight entrance she sought, she started a slow circle of the building. Rolling through two inches of water in the street speckled her pants with mud. There it was. There was an open door. And there was Joe, the security man.

"Are you Mr. Dubonnet's daughter?" he asked, holding the door behind him open with his foot.

"Yes. Joe?"

"That's me. Bring that bicycle inside. Here, let me help you."

He got her inside, where it was dark.

No human bothered the resting couple under the Expressway, but a hungry stray dog woke them up. It was what Tubby thought of as a "New Orleans yellow dog," a small lab, maybe, or part retriever, but whatever the breed he and his cousins were a common sight around town. This one had a very wet cold nose.

"Whoa!" Tubby exclaimed, jerking up. Hope caught herself from falling to the pavement.

"Back, you cur," the lawyer said pleasantly. He got to his feet and helped his friend up. They must have been passed out for an hour.

"Let's see if we can make it all the way this time," he said, offering his arm.

"Piece of cake," she replied. Eyes darting right and left to ward off the enemy, they completed the last leg of their journey. The lonesome dog followed them, tail between its legs.

There were no city policemen at the Ernest Morial Convention Center, but there was a minivan outside marked Federal Emergency Management Agency. There were aid workers wearing orange vests milling about, and helicopters hovering overhead. A big parked truck was painted with a Red Cross.

"Finally, we made it," Tubby said to one of the official-looking people. "Can we come in?"

"Keep walking, sir. You are in." The dog whined, but he got left behind.

A tall black man asked, "You got anything in that bag, sir? Drugs? Weapons?"

"No," Tubby said and kept on moving. "Who do you suppose that guy was?" Tubby asked Hope. "He didn't seem very official."

Yellow police tapes marked their path into the building.

"Excuse me, sir, this lady is a diabetic," Tubby tried to get a passing FEMA shirt to listen. The man hurried away. Hope and Tubby followed the yellow tape into a large meeting hall.

It was packed with humanity, mostly African American humanity. Babies were crying. Men pushed and shoved each other. Family groups defended their spots on the floor. Long lines snaked through the confusion.

"What's up there?" Tubby asked a man at the tail end of one of them.

"Food. MREs," the man said. "That's what I heard."

"How about medical help?"

"Somewhere in that direction," He pointed across a room as large as a football stadium teeming with people. It was sweltering in this place. Tubby could barely tolerate the throng at a Saints game. This scene was over the top. He saw a woman urinate on the floor. Hope began to sag.

No, this can't be our refuge.

"This is bedlam!" Tubby shouted. No one could hear him, for the bedlam. He stepped on an old woman's outstretched foot. She was passed out on a pink blanket.

"I'm sorry," he called. Someone shoved him from behind. He lost sight of Hope. A man was talking on a bullhorn nearby. An old man asked him if he had any cigarettes. He heard a woman scream, "Rape!" He saw Hope, down on one knee and retching, and he pushed and shoved until he reached her.

"Let's get out of here," he said.

Helping her up, he tried to retrace their steps out of the building, but they were stopped at the door.

"You can't leave, sir. This is an evacuation site. There's a mandatory evacuation. No one can be on the streets."

"I was just on the streets," Tubby protested. "They're a whole lot better than this."

"Please return to the assembly room, sir. No one is allowed to leave the building."

"I can't believe this. I'm a lawyer. You have no right to keep me here."

"Sir, if you do not return to the assembly room, I will have you forcibly restrained."

Tubby sputtered, but Hope held him tightly. "Let's go back in," she said. Her voice was so weak he could barely hear it.

"How long do we stay here?" Tubby called over his shoulder.

"Until the buses come," the official said.

Tubby and Hope squatted on the floor, people stepping all around them. He couldn't face up to the long food line. He heard someone say there wasn't any food ahead anyway. Hope's eyes were glazing over.

"Let's just see about this," he muttered, digging Flowers's cell phone out of his pocket.

He tried Flowers's number, but got a message, repeatedly, "We're sorry, all circuits are busy."

"Damn," he cursed. That's why he hadn't had one all of these years.

"Try text messaging," Hope said thinly. Her eyes were closed. "I heard you could send a text message."

"What the hell is a text message?" Tubby sputtered.

A kid with black dreadlocks, a black shirt, and an earring stuck in his lip, was splayed out next to them. He laughed.

"I can tell you that, dude," he said.

"Yeah?" Tubby was suspicious.

"Let me see your phone."

Reluctantly, he handed it over.

"Now," the kid said. "Who do you want to call?"

Tubby gave him Flowers's number.

"Now, what do you want to say?"

"Say 'I am trapped in the New Orleans Convention Center. Can you get me out of here?'"

The lad tapped on the microscopic keypad with his dirty index finger.

Bing. "Message sent," he said. He gave Tubby back his phone.

"That's it?" Tubby asked. "How will I know if he gets it?"

"Maybe he'll call you back." The kid turned over. "You're welcome," he said.

"Yeah, thank you," Tubby said contritely.

Now what to do? Leave Hope here and go stand in the food line?

His hip buzzed pleasantly. God. Some kind of nervous reaction to stress? No, it was the damn cell phone. Desperately he dug it out of his pocket and flipped it open.

"Got your message," read the little screen. "Can you get outside?"

"No," Tubby yelled. "Hey." He jostled the Goth youngster. "Look, he wants to know how to get me out. Can you send another message?"

"Look, dude," the boy said sleepily. "If I help you anymore, you've got to get me out of this, too."

"Sure." Tubby was ready to promise anything. He thrust the phone back into the kid's hand. "Tell him they won't let us out. Tell him I need some pull."

The boy went to work. It took time, as messages bounced back and forth. There were some lost attempts, when someone tripped and fell amongst them, or when the phone inexplicably refused to function, but somehow an arrangement was made.

There was a Captain Beateroff outside the building at Entrance C. He knew Flowers and was going to release Tubby Dubonnet and his party, consisting now of a woman named Hope and a youth named "Gastro," make that Sydney Peavy, from the "evacuation headquarters" for pick-up by one certain detective named Sanre Fueres. Their mission was to get to said Entrance C in half an hour.

Tubby organized his crew. Gastro checked his socks and pockets to make sure his possessions were still there, a few bucks and a turquoise ring he had scrounged off the Convention Center floor in the dark. They set off into the crowd.

"Like a mosh pit," Gastro remarked.

It wasn't easy. They almost got discouraged and failed, but with perseverance they achieved their objective.

"Officer Beateroff!" they all screamed in unison.

12

ETECTIVE FLOWERS WAS WAITING FOR THEM AT THE skirmish line hastily erected by FEMA and the Department of Wild Life and Fisheries to keep people in. He was leaned up against a white Ford 350 crew-cab with a sign plastered on the side: DISASTER RELIEF. DO NOT DELAY. He had on black slacks, a crisp blue shirt with a "Superior Security Services" patch on the shoulder, and a gun belt. He was joking with an NOPD officer wearing camouflage fatigues tucked into his combat boots. Tubby and his party cried for attention, and Flowers interrupted his conversation to wave them through.

"Thank God." Tubby shook Flowers's hand and hugged him. "These are my people." He introduced Hope and Sid "Gastro" Peavy. A dog nudged his leg. "This one, too," Tubby said.

The cops couldn't care less what happened to anybody once they were checked out of the building, so there was absolutely no hassle. The refugees scrambled into the super-sized truck, and Flowers climbed in behind the wheel.

"Was it kind of rough in there?" he asked.

"You wouldn't believe it!" Tubby exclaimed. "We need to call the Governor or something to get those people out of there. It is totally inhumane. It's like . . ." Words failed him.

"It's totally like taking a crap on the floor with like a million of your best friends, while sick people are dying around you," Gastro finished for him.

"We're thankful for your help, Mr. Flowers," Hope told him. "It really is terrible in there. Those poor people . . ." The dog nudged her chin and cut her off.

"This entire city is in terrible shape," Flowers said grimly. "I didn't know how bad until I drove in to get you. I mean, there was plenty of wind damage out where we're going in Kenner, and I can pick up some of the news on the radio, but I didn't realize how big the flood got."

He was taking them away from the downtown area. Tchoupitoulas Street was deserted, and he sped around fragments of chimneys and, oddly, an overturned basketball goal on the roadway. A pack of dogs dashed in front of them and raced toward the wharves. Their canine companion in the truck barked enthusiastically.

"Let's call him 'Lucky,'" Hope suggested.

"Not yet lucky," Gastro said. "Please get your nose out of my face, Not Yet Lucky."

CHRISTINE WAS IN the office tower's elevator with Bonner Rivette before she realized that something was wrong. A red emergency light dimly illuminated the walnut-paneled box, and she could see that his mismatched sports coat and pants just did not correlate at all to what a security man's uniform ought to look like. Rivette stared at her, and he didn't smile. She picked her knapsack of groceries off the floor and clutched it in her arms.

"Where is my father?" she asked.

The elevator reached floor 43, and the door slid open.

She balked at leaving.

"He's in his office," Bonner told her.

Warily Christine stepped in the hall.

"Right there," Bonner said, pointing.

She straightened her shoulders and marched to the big glass doors, which were standing open. Exit signs lit the hall.

When she reached the office reception area she swung around to confront the man. Her jaw was set, but she couldn't speak.

"He ain't really here," Bonner said. "I made that up."

She snarled and swung her pack at him. He caught it in one hand and reeled her in.

FLOWERS AND HIS EXPANDED RETINUE arrived safely at the Petrofoods complex in the remote end of Jefferson Parish known as Kenner. They were out by the airport, and as far as you could go without falling into a swamp. At Petrofoods there was a two-story administration building and warehouse, a garage for equipment and trucks, a bunker for helicopter maintenance, and a large concrete landing field, all surrounded by a chain link fence. The fence was topped with barbed wire. The site had once been a military installation and was rumored to have played a role in the Bay of Pigs invasion.

"What do they do here?" Tubby asked, looking at all the fences.

"Petrofoods is a supply company for off-shore oil rigs," Flowers explained. "Everything from canned goods and frozen rib-eyes to hand tools and electrical wire. They've got a bigger facility in Lafayette, and that's where the company is operating from this week. Once they get the juice turned back on here, they'll move back in."

"You're here all by yourself?"

"Not quite." Flowers rocketed the big Ford into the "No Parking" space in front of the main building. There was only one other truck on the lot, a beat-up Nissan Frontier with the tailgate missing. The Airodream helicopter Tubby had ridden in rested some distance away, its props wilted in sleep. The flight control tower of the Louis Armstrong Airport was visible half a mile off. For the time being at least, the airport was totally out of business. Tubby wondered how many tourists were stranded in the terminal. He imagined that they were being well cared for, but he was wrong.

"I've got a young guy, Steve Oubre, with me," Flowers said. "I don't think you ever met him. I only hired him last June . . . He's just a good ol' Cajun. And we had a visit yesterday from one of the company wheels. A vice president of something. He came to check on us and then go look at his house. He didn't come back. Me and Steve are in charge here until told otherwise."

Everybody got out of the truck, and the dog ran off to pee. Flowers took Hope by the elbow. "Let me show you the accommodations," he said gallantly.

He led them into the company office, a bunch of empty desks and filing cabinets. Family pictures and little plastic flowers adorned the desktops, all left behind in the hurry to evacuate. In the back was the warehouse, a huge space full of floor-to-ceiling shelves, packed with merchandise. The electricity was off, and the available light came from an overhead door cranked open at the rear of the building.

They followed the light, past gallon cans of cheese sauce, bottles of apple juice, cases of flashlights, and cartons of instant grits. Near the back door, cots had been laid out. A large barbecue grill made from a fifty-five-gallon drum occupied center stage, and smoke drifted from under the lid. A generator droned outside. A young bearded man sat on a blue nylon folding chair watching a small television set and smoking a cigarette. He clicked off the set, on which he had a "Stepford Wives II" DVD playing, and got up to say hello.

"This is Steve." Flowers made introductions. "Find some more cots for these folks," he ordered. "Put the lady's somewhere over there by those bags of plastic plates. See if you can find any more blankets. How are the ribs coming along?"

"Man, they're looking good," Steve said. He shook hands with everybody, including Gastro, whom he studied with keen interest, looking the black-clad youth up and down. "You got more earrings than I got," he said. Indeed Gastro had two in the tops of each ear and one in his lip, for a total of five. Steve only had one, and it was through his left earlobe.

Gastro shrugged, not sure how to take it.

"The girls like that, huh?' Steve asked.

"Seem to," Gastro said.

"That's good. Let me see how many cots I can find."

"We're eating okay," Flowers explained, an understatement. "There's lots in the reefer truck, which is hooked to the generator. Are y'all hungry? Just give me ten minutes," the dark-haired detective promised.

Everybody was beyond hungry. With Steve's help, Flowers set out a feast on a plastic folding table. It consisted of canned beans and cheese sauce, creamed potatoes from a three-pound pouch, a pan of biscuits, a pot of hot coffee, cantaloupe slices from the refrigerator truck, and a platter of steaming hot tamales. "The ribs need another hour," he explained. They didn't care.

When round one of the meal was finished, Hope asked to see her cot, and Steve showed her the spot he'd selected between stacks of styrofoam cups and disposable cereal bowls. Gastro said he needed a walk, and Flowers said he could go anywhere, but to stay out of the office and keep away from the helicopter.

"I've got a bottle of rum," he confided to Tubby. "And a Coke." He fixed them each a drink in sixteen-ounce plastic cups.

The dog, full of leftover tamales and biscuits, lay at their feet expelling gas. "What are you going to call that thing?" Flowers asked.

"I don't know. Hope said 'Lucky' and the street urchin said 'Not Yet.' If I name him I have to keep him."

"I think he's keeping you."

"I believe he likes you better. You name him."

"How about 'Windy'?"

"How about 'Rex'?"

"Rex it is," Flowers said. "The king of our carnival. And you named him."

TUBBY WOKE UP in his chair about two o'clock in the morning. The grill, cleared of its rack of ribs, now was serving as a sort of campfire fueled by chunks of broken fork-lift pallets. Gastro and Steve were still sitting around it, jawing. Tubby suspected they had found some beer or pot. The radio was turned low and alternated between country music and news. He listened to their conversation for a minute.

"It's not that easy living on the streets," Gastro was saying.

"Not easy in what way? You don't pay no rent. You don't work." Steve burped, but he was interested in what Gastro had to say.

"I work," Gastro said defensively. "I'm an oyster shucker by trade. But I got fired. And I do day labor, clean up trash, stuff like that. But you know the cops hassle you. And there's a lot of sicko people out there." He had, in fact, found little kindness in life, and when someone mentioned that concept he thought they were hustling him.

"Then why don't you get off those streets and get you some place to live?" Steve asked.

"It's not that easy. You've got to have rent money, and they want a security deposit. You've got to sign a lease. Man, I don't know where I'll be next week."

"That's for sure, these days," Steve said. "Don't you have no family you can turn to?"

"Not really. They don't want anything to do with me."

"True? I've known some people like that. What don't they like about you?"

"Because of the way I dress and who I am."

"I guess you can't be anybody but who you are," Steve said sagely. " I had a cousin who tried to pretend he was a race car driver but he was really a forklift operator. He killed himself driving his forklift off the pier at the Port Sulphur Marina."

"I see what you mean," Gastro said thoughtfully. "Is that where you're from, Port Sulphur?"

"That's where I'm from. My daddy's from Lake Charles, but we lived in Port Sulphur since I was ten. It ain't much. Port Sulphur," Steve concluded.

"I've never been there," Gastro said. Since coming to New Orleans from Montgomery, Alabama, he had never been anywhere but the French Quarter.

Their conversation was putting Tubby back to sleep, but before he drifted away he caught a little of the voice on the radio. The reporter was saying there was widespread looting throughout New Orleans. The flooding had stopped, but the police were deserting. Some were even caught on camera stealing from stores. The mayor was demanding to know when federal troops would arrive. He said there were thousands of dead bodies floating around the city.

It was hard to sleep through that. Tubby found himself missing his good friend Raisin, who had stayed behind in Bolivia to finish off their business there. No telling when he would see Raisin again. The man spoke almost no Spanish but had a way of making himself understood in any language, and he had enough money to get through the month if he didn't waste it all on women and high-priced booze. Man, a shot of good whiskey cost forty Bolivianos in the ex-pat bars. And beer was high, too, if you wanted it cold. It would be good to have Raisin around New Orleans right now. He could take care of himself, and then some. Tubby wished he could turn back the clock. He hoped all of his kids were safe.

13

CHRISTINE WAS STILL ALIVE, BUT SHE WAS NOT SURE FOR how much longer. Bonner had slapped her around until she quit fighting. He had threatened to throw her out the window. He had wrestled her to the floor. She thought he would break her arms. She had tried to hit him with a crystal paperweight, and he twisted her hair in his strong hands until her eyes almost popped out. Violating her sexually did not seem to be his goal.

When she finally gave up, he did too.

Rivette was quiet now. He squatted on the carpet by one of the picture windows. Past him Christine could see the stars. He had a pair of scissors and was fashioning what appeared to be a doily, or a string of paper dolls.

"I am Katrina," he had whispered into her ear while he had her pinned face down on her father's desk.

She inched her way across the carpet, hoping to get out of the room.

"You can't leave," he said simply.

She stopped, afraid to speak.

"People shouldn't live like this. It's not supposed to be this way."

He went back to his scissors and paper.

"Uh," she tried tentatively. "What do you mean?"

He set his project aside and faced her, crossing his arms over his knees.

"Boxes, cages, buildings, jails. It's all wrong. It's all got to come down."

"Why does it have to come down?" she forced herself to ask. At her college orientation, where they lectured on the dangers in the big city, the social workers always advised, "Keep 'em talking."

"The hurricane and me are just alike," Rivette said thoughtfully. "We're clearing the table. The way the hurricane blew things apart here and moved on was great," he mused, "but part of me stayed."

"Part of what stayed?"

"Part of the hurricane is part of me." Bonner's thoughts were a little confused, but he was putting the pieces together.

"You're just a person," Christine whispered. "No one is a hurricane."

"Wrong," he said.

She calculated the distance to the door.

Rivette seemed to sense this and became more alert.

"You probably wouldn't understand," he continued, "but we can get lots of power from the hurricane if we let it get inside us."

"How would that be exactly? The hurricane is a part of nature, and you're just a man."

"I'm more than that. You could be more than that, too."

A crazy thought hit Christine. This lunatic who had slammed her around wanted a soul-mate. Someone to share his world. She didn't know what that world was, and she didn't want a ticket to find out.

She tried a different approach. "Katrina is free as the wind," Christine argued, "and you're stuck in this little room."

He didn't like that.

"I've been stuck in lots worse places, and I always get out."

After a minute he said, "You can come along if you want."

"To do what?" she asked.

"To get stronger," he said. "Like right now. I've been meditating and getting stronger and freer."

"Maybe we'd get stronger quicker if we'd just call the rescue people and have them get us out of here."

"I'm not stupid, you know, Christine."

"You keep saying my name," she said. "What's yours?"

Bonner didn't answer. He was deep in jumbled thought. His spiritual aim, gleaned from reading some crumbling religious pamphlets his uncle kept in a cigar box, was loss of human form. This was assisted by meditation, and also by eating fruit, but Rivette didn't have any fruit. The hurricane had been so strong and free. Where could such a power have come from? He'd like to find out. And even in the spirit world, there was usually a male and a female. Perhaps that would explain why this female attracted him so.

She interrupted his reverie. "I don't think you're getting freer sitting here," she said. "I think your spirit is in a cage."

Christine was unaware of the destructive potential of Rivette's spirit, but she nevertheless plowed ahead. She had been raised to be a good arguer.

"No one who does evil is free," she told him.

She got off the floor and sat on the desk and adjusted her blouse. When she wiped her cheek she saw there was blood on her fingers. She rubbed it off on her jeans.

"What are you, some kind of a Sunday school teacher?"

"No, but there's got to be something better you could be doing with your strength than beating up on women."

"I didn't hit you to hurt you," he said, turning away. She calculated her chances of getting out the door, reaching the dark hallway, and hiding somewhere in the building. They weren't very good.

"Really? Well, why did you then? You see I'm bleeding."

"I'm sorry," he said, and he did regret it. "It wouldn't have hurt if you knew about the periculum, the per-ga, the ro-wero."

She thought he might be speaking in tongues like some TV evangelist.

"What do those words mean?" she inquired.

"It's protection, it's power, it's Scythian," he explained earnestly.

"That's what you tap into?"

"That's what I tap into."

"Don't you think there's something more creative you could tap into? How about relating to other people in a normal way?"

Something was wrong with that statement. The criminal's face went hard and she could almost watch him go back over to the dark side. He crossed the room and planted himself with his back to the door, the only way out. "You stay here," he said and closed his eyes. In his mind he traveled somewhere else.

CHRISTINE BECAME CONSCIOUS that she was alive and that she had been sleeping. She was lying on the carpet. A few feet away Rivette sat in a chair, staring out the window at the sun coming up.

"What you said about 'creative,' what did you mean?" he asked.

She was slightly delirious, but she struggled to make her mind work. "Creative. Opening your eyes to the world. Bringing things to life."

"There are different kinds of life," he said. "Human life ain't much."

"Have you given it a chance?" Christine asked. Her body ached all over. Just stay alive, she thought. I am with a very disturbed person.

Rivette didn't respond, but his pointy chin dropped to his chest. Just when she thought he might be drifting off he jerked upright and stared at her imploringly, like a dog begging for a bone.

"What's your real name, anyway?" she asked, encouraging him.

"I told you."

"Katrina? No, I mean your real name."

He smiled. "Bonner," he said. "Bonner Rivette."

"Okay, Bonner. Don't you care about your own life? Don't you think you'd better fly out of here before you get caught?"

He nodded his head.

"Why don't you call my father? He can help."

"Right." He looked into his cupped palms like he was reading a book.

"I'm serious. He's a lawyer. He can pull strings."

"You talk like I'm crazy."

She forced a laugh. "You and me, we had a fight. We're sort of like brothers and sisters now. What are we supposed to do? Jump off the building? I want to live, too. Let's get out of here together. He won't call the police or anything. Not if I ask him not to. He's got a car. You could probably have it. He'd do that in a minute to rescue me."

Bonner cocked his head and looked into her eyes. He was reflecting upon the proposition.

FLOWERS TOOK TUBBY up for a flight in the Airodream early on Thursday morning. According to the radio, the National Guard might arrive today, but they saw no signs of it. Other helicopters buzzed around—one was a big orange Coast Guard bird that Tubby recognized as the distraction beating its props the last couple of years over Mardi Gras parades. Another was from a TV station. There was a black one, flying straight over the city on a serious mission, with HOMELAND SECURITY stenciled on its side. He and Flowers, in their small noisy craft, buzzed over the famous break in the Seventeenth Street Canal levee, which they had heard about on the radio but which neither of them had seen.

It was about a hundred yards long, right up close to the lake, on the New Orleans side of a canal that ran about three miles. Its purpose was to drain street run-off into Lake Pontchartrain from a wide swath of the metropolitan area. It separated New Orleans from the adjoining parish. Its point of origin was way back around the Metairie Cemetery, and it was fed all the way by big pumping stations on both sides of the city line. Hurricane Katrina had filled the lake like the world's biggest hot tub, and its waters had sloshed around in the canal long enough to find an unexpectedly soft dike. The break was about fifty feet from the back doors of a whole block of upper middle-class urbanites. The water lifted their swimming pools and decks out of the ground, uprooted their trees, and swept their houses across several streets. Then it engulfed another hundred thousand homes.

Down below Flowers and Tubby they could see men with hard hats milling about on the fringes of the breach, studying the problem. Water from the lake was still washing through.

"Wonder why they can't just drop a few eighteen-wheelers into that breach until they get it plugged?" Flowers asked.

"Must not be in the plan," Tubby offered.

"I doubt they ever had a plan."

"Criminal stupidity," Tubby muttered.

Roofs and chimneys poked through the flood like lilies in an endless pond.

"Lord have mercy," Flowers said. "Look how far that water has spread."

They clattered over to the New Orleans side of the breach. As far as their eyes could take them, the lake had reclaimed the city for itself.

"It goes on for miles," Tubby said, looking at the isolated rooftops of whole neighborhoods he was quite familiar with, Lakeview, Lake Vista, Gentilly, Mid-City, Carrollton, Old Metairie.

"You see those people down there?" Flowers asked.

"You mean the engineer types? Yeah, I saw them and I wonder why they're not up here with us dropping railroad cars full of sand into that hole. How dumb do you have to be . . ."

"No, I mean those people on the roofs."

Tubby looked down, and indeed there were clusters of people on several roofs, right below where he guessed Fleur de Lis Avenue might have been. "You want to rescue them?" he asked.

"I don't see any place to put down," Flowers cried, but he was already fluttering lower.

"Could I go down on a rope?"

"Yes and no. There's a lanyard and a saddle behind you, but the winch may not be strong enough to pull you back up."

"Let's try it and see." While the prop wash animated the tree tops below, Tubby scrounged around the tiny compartment behind his seat and organized the ropes. He tested the electric winch, and it buzzed to life.

"Seems to be okay," he said. He strapped himself into the saddle. He opened the hatch door on the deck.

"You sure you want to try this?" Flowers asked doubtfully. "You ain't no young stud." One hundred feet under the skids, a woman in a chenille bathrobe waved at them frantically, trying to stand on steeply pitched shingles.

"Just get me as close as you can," Tubby said. "I happen to be a former rugby player." He had seen heroes do this on television before, and he felt heroic, having survived the Convention Center.

It also seemed that the world had revolved many a time since he had last practiced law.

Flowers put the bird about forty feet above the woman, who was shouting at them. Some kind of creature was on the roof with her. It was a small dog, yapping and trying to keep its footing.

"Geronimo." Tubby smiled and eased himself through the hatch. He climbed onto the strut while Flowers fought to keep the Airodream level. The winch gave him slack. He let his feet dangle, then slid his legs into space. For a minute he held onto the strut as if it were a trapeze bar, then let go. He swung in the wind, and the winch slowly lowered him down. When his feet hit the roof he stumbled and would have toppled into the water lapping the gutters if he hadn't been tugged up short by the lanyard around his waist and shoulders.

The woman understood that they were trying to rescue her, but she didn't know what to do. The dog was frantically skittering from one end of the roof to the other.

Teetering on the slope, Tubby unbuckled himself carefully, deafened by the rotor noise. The woman looked like his sweet old Aunt Nellie, if Aunt Nellie had been left out in the sun to cook for a couple of days. Her rosette face radiated hope when he approached with the contraption, and she feigned modesty when he fastened it around her legs and waist.

"What about Pookie?" she asked sweetly in his ear. "I can't leave without Pookie."

"Okay." Tubby crawled on his knees along the crown of the roof. "Here, Pookie," he sang. The dog was not cooperating. She retreated along the ridge tiles then feinted left and ran right to get around this strange intruder. She momentarily lost her footing and almost plopped into the water, but at the last second she clawed her way back to the top and scampered to her owner. The woman made the catch and gathered Pookie to her breast.

"Up you go," Tubby said, and he made his thumbs up to Flowers.

The winch jerked the woman about two feet off the roof. She screamed and Pookie went flying. The dog landed on the pitched shingles and listlessly wobbled closer to her doom. The screaming woman was pulled higher and higher.

"Here, Pookie," Tubby called desperately. Looking up he saw the woman's bedroom slippers disappear into the helicopter. On his rump he slid toward the dog, but too late. It flopped into the gray-green chop.

The sudden bath seemed to energize the dog, however, and Pookie flailed at the drip edge until she found purchase. As if pursued by frenzied hounds she clawed her way straight up the roof and hopped into Tubby's arms.

"You are one smelly critter," he said happily.

The dog remained attached to Tubby while the rope and saddle came back down and as he clumsily used his other hand to get himself buckled in. When that mission was accomplished he signaled Flowers. The line went taut, lifting Tubby to his tip-toes, and then stopped.

Inside the helicopter, the woman wanted to know if that man had her little darling. Flowers was cursing at the winch.

"You're too damn big." Flowers shouted. "You weigh too much for this blamed ..." He tried the winch again, and it groaned tiredly. Flowers looked down at Tubby looking up at him. "This should be fun," he frowned. He pulled the handle and the Airo-dream ascended, swinging its human cargo forty feet below.

"Yaaah!" Tubby cried, watching chimneys and the tops of cypress trees pass below his feet. He clutched Pookie tightly for protection. "Yaaah!" They crossed the Seventeenth Street Canal, and the men in hard hats stared up at him shielding their eyes with their hands. He had a fine view of the lake and the wet churches and apartments on Metairie Road, when he dared to open his eyes. This wasn't so bad.

He twirled slowly and thought it was sort of like the time he was in the revolving bar at the World Trade Center. He took in the landscape of missing roofs and toppled billboards. Behind him was New Orleans. Over there was the sublimely peaceful Lake Pontchartrain. The fine homes and golf courses of Old Metairie had flooded. Now that was interesting. Where was Flowers taking him?

To Lakeside Shopping Center, it turned out. Right by JCPenney's. Right down to the big parking lot. Gently, Tubby's feet touched the ground. Flowers brought it a little lower, and Tubby could get out of the harness. He had to sit on the pavement, keeping his grip on the dog. Once he was inert, the copter could move away to land. The woman took her time getting out, and shook herself like a bird ruffling its feathers. When she felt sufficiently composed she ran across the parking lot. Flowers hurried behind her, coming to check on his human yo-yo.

"Pookie," the woman cried. She had to peel the dog out of Tubby's arms, and when she had her furry love she showered it with kisses.

"Are you all right, boss?" Flowers asked, poking Tubby's shoulder to get a reaction.

"I'm fine." He couldn't move yet. "Just a little windblown. Can you help me up?"

Flowers helped them all get straightened out. "I saw a police check-point at the other side of the shopping center when we came down," he said. "I'll run over there and see if they'll take this woman somewhere."

While Flowers was gone, Tubby and the woman walked in little circles, getting used to being alive and safe.

"What's your name?" the lady asked.

Tubby told her.

"Mine's Theresa Campbell, and I've never been in one of them things before."

"How long had you been on that roof?" Tubby asked.

"I'm not sure, what day is this?"

"Thursday, I think."

"Then two days. I was up in the attic for one day, I'm pretty sure. And then I figured no one was going to find me there. If I wanted to keep living, I'd have to get where someone could see me. And here I am," she said with satisfaction.

"And here you are. How'd you get out of the attic?"

"Why, I had to knock out a little window in the front of my house and swim for it. It was a pretty stained-glass window, but I guess we can't worry about things like that now."

"I guess not. Why didn't you evacuate ahead of the storm?"

"I didn't expect this," she said simply. "And I love my little house. Isn't that right, Pookie? Mama almost got us both drowned."

Flowers rode back in a Jefferson Parish Sheriff's car. They loaded Ms. Campbell and her dog and took them away.

"Are you all right, man?" Flowers asked Tubby. "You look a little seasick."

"You try riding in that saddle. They ought to turn it into some kind of Olympic event— Yow!"

His pocket was buzzing. Tubby dug out the cell phone, surprised that it worked.

He listened a second.

"Yes, this is Tubby Dubonnet. Who is this?"

"Let me speak to her."

"Hello, Christine?"

"How're you doing, baby? Tell me what's wrong."

"Say it again. Where are you?"

"Hey, put my daughter back on."

"Yes, of course I understand. And listen, if she gets hurt in the least . . . hello? Hello?"

Tubby snapped the phone shut.

"Some guy has kidnapped Christine," he told Flowers.

"Say that again?"

"He's got her at my office downtown, and she says I should come and get her."

"Who is this guy?"

"I have no idea. I didn't recognize his voice. He just sounded . . . cold."

"Then let's go get her."

"He didn't say what he wanted with me."

"Maybe money."

"He didn't ask for money."

"So we should fly the bird back downtown?"

Tubby nodded his head. Together they trotted back to the tired helicopter.

14

THE GREAT PAN OF NEW ORLEANS HAD TURNED UPSIDE down. From the sky, it was a shock to see. The flood waters, bright emerald where they flowed in from the lake through the breaches, became as brown as desert sands as they spread for miles through the neighborhoods, absorbing the sediment of civilization. The treetops, always green in New Orleans, had likewise turned brown from the stress of hundred mile per hour winds or airborne salt. Tubby's mood was likewise brown, from fatigue and anxiety. They shared the sky with a dozen other helicopters, hell bent on missions of their own.

"No gulls," Flowers observed.

"Huh?"

"You always watch for birds around here when you fly these things. Seagulls, ducks, cormorants, whatever. There aren't any birds."

"Must have blown away," Tubby said.

"Must have. I'm going to set this down on top of the building again, right?"

"Yeah," Tubby told him. "I don't know if you should even get out. We may need to make a quick getaway. You know, I left my .45 back at Petrofoods."

"Don't worry. I've got plenty of firepower," Flowers said. "You want a gun?"

"No, you should keep it. I'm so excited I'd shoot myself."

"I don't think guns are your style anyway, boss. There's some kind of knife in the kit box there. Help yourself if you want."

Tubby checked and found a worn Uncle Henry pocket knife. He remembered these from his youth, growing up in north Louisiana. "Guaranteed against loss," he reminisced. "I guess I will take that."

"What's the plan?" Flowers asked.

"I don't have one. He just said he had her, come get her. I suppose he's an intelligent person who wants something in exchange. I'm sure he's not interested in surrendering to us. Perhaps it's cash."

"Do you have any?"

"I got a couple of hundred. Then there's checks and credit cards, but that probably won't help us."

"I've got a few bucks, too," Flowers said. "But maybe we can arrange for him to fall off the building."

They set down on the roof, cut the motor, and disembarked. Tubby tried the door, but it was locked. Now what?

"Call them on the cell phone," Flowers instructed.

Tubby did, having trouble mashing the right buttons with his big fingers. Christine answered right away.

"How are you?" he asked immediately.

"I'm okay. I'm okay," she reassured him.

"We're on the roof," Tubby told her.

"Of the building?"

"Yes."

Tubby could hear the muffled voices as she reported this to her captor.

"He wants to know why you're on the roof."

"We have a helicopter."

More garbled voices.

"He wants to know who is up there with you."

"Just me and the pilot. No police or anything. It's the only way I could get down here. I can't get to my car." Another pause.

"He says that's okay. Just wait for us. And I think everything will be cool if you guys are cool."

"We'll be very cool," Tubby said.

"They're coming up," he told Flowers. "We're supposed to be cool."

Flowers nodded. He leaned out the hatch of the Airodream, looking cool. Tubby hopped around nervously, fingering the Uncle Henry knife in his pocket.

Finally the metal door from the stairwell opened a crack. After a moment while someone concealed inside obviously inspected the surroundings, the door creaked open wider, and Christine came out. She was wearing a collar, made of a leather belt, and the man who appeared behind her had the end of the belt in one hand and a gun in the other. The weapon had belonged to Manuel, the security man, but now it was Bonner Rivette's.

Tubby's eyes closed to slits as he watched his daughter and the thug approach. Ten feet away, Rivette jerked Christine to a halt, which caused her head to snap back. Pointing his gun at her ear, he took his time looking around the roof for hidden danger.

"Who's Dubonnet?" he asked.

Tubby identified himself. "What do you want?"

"Out of here. Are you the pilot?" he asked Flowers.

Flowers nodded.

"Let's fly away then," Bonner said. He nudged Christine in the direction of the Airodream.

"Wait just a minute," Tubby demanded. "She stays here."

Rivette lowered the gun and targeted the lawyer's midsection.

Tubby studied the man intently and saw hot blank eyes, like an alligator's or a cornered raccoon's, staring back at him. "No. She goes with me," Rivette said.

"Then I guess you know how to fly this thing?" Flowers interjected. "Because I follow Mr. Dubonnet's orders."

"She goes with me," Rivette insisted. "Take me where I tell you to and I'll let her go. Otherwise let's get it on right here."

"Who are you?" Tubby asked.

"His name is Bonner Rivette," Christine said loudly.

Rivette jerked the leash again. "No fair giving away my secrets," he said. "I am who I am. Your daughter will be safe with me."

"Take that leash off her," Tubby said.

"Once we're all in the helicopter, I might."

"Okay, let's all get in," Tubby said.

Bonner pushed Christine toward the hatch.

"Can you help me out of a legal jam?" he asked Tubby in all seriousness, though he was holding the lawyer's daughter on a leash.

Daddy didn't miss a beat. "Quite possibly," he said. "What's the charge?"

"Assault and kidnapping."

"I'm a witness to that. I can't be your lawyer," Tubby said automatically.

"Then I don't need you. He stays here," he told Flowers.

"Like hell," Tubby said.

"Hey, boss," Flowers called. "I'm not sure this baby can carry us all anyway."

"This is no good," Tubby objected. "I can't sit here while this man flies off with my daughter."

"You ain't got a choice," the criminal said.

"I'll take care of her," Flowers promised. "And I won't forget you here."

The criminal pushed Christine into the helicopter.

"Wait a second!" Tubby yelled.

Flowers started the blades whirling. The lawyer saw the gun pointed at his daughter's head. He protested some more. The Airodream began to lift off. Christine mouthed, "I love you . . ."

Tubby ran for the helicopter and tried to jump aboard, but Rivette's foot caught him in the chin and he fell backwards. Flowers rattled higher, and Tubby watched them go where he could not follow.

He gripped his Uncle Henry knife helplessly in his fist.

The helicopter swung toward the south and flew away, into the sky from whence Hurricane Katrina had come.

15

TUBBY KNEW HE HAD NOT BEEN A PERFECT FATHER. HE had made mistakes, though sitting on a roof forty-nine flights up, he couldn't actually think of any. Well, there was the time he had passed out on Christmas Eve, but how minor was that? He had worked hard, in spurts, and provided for the family. He should have spent more time with the girls. Well, in all honesty, he had spent a lot of time with Debbie, the oldest. He had taken her to Tulane football games and helped her with her homework, because she needed it. And Debbie had gotten pregnant and then married, so he had a grandchild, and he just seemed to see a lot of Debbie.

And of course, Monique, the youngest, was so darn pretty and inquisitive that he had always found it easy to spend time just talking to her. But Christine was right in the middle, and maybe he had let her down. Christine always seemed to be in charge, and in a way she took after her mother. Not her mother's bad traits, which in Tubby's mind included being whiny, disloyal, irresponsible and greedy, but the good traits like being strong-willed, and self-confident, and determined to get what she wanted out of life. He had just taken Christine for granted, he told himself. Such a wonderful child. He should have protected her more.

Peering into the empty sky where the helicopter had disappeared, he tried praying.

The Airodream came back just before dark.

Tubby jumped up and waited anxiously for Flowers to land and report on what had happened. When the helicopter settled on the roof, Tubby rushed forward and grabbed his friend's arm even before the props were still, and he would have physically squeezed words out of the detective had he not suddenly seen Christine anxiously reaching for him in the passenger seat.

She smiled when she stumbled out of the hatch. Father and daughter ran together and hugged. Tubby smoothed her hair down the back of her neck and cried.

When they were all back at the Petrofoods warehouse Tubby drew Christine aside into an aisle of canned green beans and potato chips.

"What did he do to you?" he asked.

"Nothing, Daddy, we just fought."

"Did he hit you? Did he hurt you? Your face is bruised."

"Yes, he hit me, but I'm okay."

"Should we go to a doctor?"

"Where would we find one?" she spread out her hands to make the point.

"We have a helicopter. We have trucks. We can find a doctor."

"I'll be okay." She turned away.

"You're not telling me everything!" He was exasperated. He wanted to crush a gallon of green beans like Popeye crushed spinach.

"I'm very hungry," she told him.

"I'm going to going to get that man," Tubby promised her.

"Let's rest now," she said.

"Okay," he conceded, but he was wondering where she got such inner strength.

She was thinking, I've got to protect Daddy or else he'll get himself killed protecting me.

Sitting around the campfire-in-a grill tended by Steve, Christine told some of her story. Flowers was out on the lot, gassing up his ride. He had finally taken off his sunglasses. The night was peaceful.

Wood smoke blew through the warehouse. Steve had planks of frozen rib-eyes in plastic packages defrosting. Hope Lestella and Gastro had been mixing the ingredients for an industrial-size coconut cake to be baked in an aluminum turkey pan all courtesy of the Petrofoods company, but they stopped when Christine emerged from the "field shower." It consisted of a bench and plastic jugs of water surrounded by a tarp. She looked refreshed and ready to talk. Tubby had sat down on a lawn chair with his eyes closed, and he was nursing a cup of Flowers's rum.

Christine took the chair Steve offered and accepted a handful of smoked almonds from the gallon jar they had opened.

"It wasn't too bad, once the fighting stopped. I'm not going into that right now. I'm the one who told Rivette to call my father. It turned out to be the only good idea I had. So when we got into the helicopter, Flowers asked Rivette where he wanted to go. He said he just wanted to get away from the flood.

"We went out to, like, Metairie, and Flowers said he wanted to land at Lakeside Shopping Center, but Bonner suspected a trick. He told Flowers to fly him all the way out of town. Flowers said he didn't have that much fuel, but he would take him down by the levee.

"So we flew over to the river, where there's nothing but trees between the levee and the bank. Bonner said it looked okay, he'd tell Flowers when to stop. We flew almost to the Huey Long Bridge before Bonner saw a place he wanted to be put down. We landed right on top of the levee in the grass where they have that bike trail, and Bonner jumps out. He still had his belt around my neck, and he tried to yank me after him. Flowers suddenly pulls out this gun and shoots right at Bonner.

"Bonner ducked, but he had to let go of me, and Flowers pulled me back into the helicopter. I felt like I was in the middle of a tug of war. Bonner shot at us, too, but Flowers got the helicopter off the ground, and we could see Bonner running into the woods. And Flowers flew after him with the helicopter and kept shooting at him, but he kept missing. I told him to stop. Just let him go. Bonner got under the trees, and we couldn't see him anymore. So then Flowers turned around and took us back to get Daddy. And then we all flew back here."

"Shouldn't you see a doctor, dear?" Hope asked.

"No. I'm all right," Christine said. Tubby heaved himself out of his chair and went to take her hand.

"You're sure?" he asked. "You don't look so hot." Her face was bruised.

"I'll be okay, Dad," she said. "I think I did everything I was supposed to." She was starting to stutter a little, like she was cold.

"Yes you did, honey." He hugged her again. "We'll eat some supper and you can get a good night's rest. I'm going to track that son of a bitch down and . . ."

"You'd better leave him alone, Daddy. He can be very mean, and I think he was telling the truth about killing people."

"How you gonna find him anyway?" Steve asked.

Tubby kept those thoughts to himself. He went outside to stare at the stars and the red running lights of helicopters streaking through the skies on their missions of mercy. Was the President up there among them, he wondered, bringing help?

"You had it rough," Gastro said to Christine. He was touched by this pretty, resilient girl with blonde hair and a serious face. She was tall and looked physically strong, like his mother. Gastro had lived on the streets since his mother died and his father kicked him out, and he thought he knew how rough, indeed, life could be. To make it in New Orleans, you had to be tough. This girl he saw as a contender.

"I bet you never thought you would have such a day as this," Steve Oubre said. He was a friendly, red-headed giant from the country, and he liked overalls. His limited experience in New Orleans had led him to believe that all the white people in the city were rich and powerful and unaccustomed to having bad things happen to them.

"It's been kind of humiliating," she whispered. And no one could think of anything to say about that.

The crew made a good meal of the steaks, under a full moon and the Milky Way. You never saw that in the city, not for a hundred years, but now the city was turned off, and the stars could shine again. They blazed across the sky. Some more rum appeared, and they all passed around the bottle and the cans of Coke. Steve kept tossing pieces of busted pallets on the fire, and he found a guitar somewhere. It turned out that Flowers, properly encouraged, could even play a little.

"I only know a couple of songs," he admitted modestly, and strummed out a decent version of "Guantanamera." And he sang, softly,

"*Yo soy un hombre sincero,*

"From the land of the palm trees,

"And before dying

"I want to share these poems of my soul.

"My poems are soft green.

"My poems are also flaming crimson.

"My poems are like a wounded fawn

"Seeking refuge in the forest.

"With the poor people of the land

"I want to share my fate.

"The streambed of the mountain

"Pleases me more than the sea. . ."

Steve hummed along and Hope joined in on the chorus. Gastro tried to find the beat.

Flowers received their applause when he was finished.

"That was José Martí. How about some Radiators?" Flowers asked and got their enthusiastic consent.

"There's no life, like that low life," he crooned. "And that low life, it's a wild life."

They got down with that.

THEY SET UP COTS for Christine and Hope off in the nacho cheese aisle, and there were plenty of blankets fresh out of the package, still smelling of the Chinese factory perfume. Christine crawled under the covers and was out like a light.

Hope lay still, looking at the ceiling, her mind full of chaotic visions of the past few days. She wondered what had become of her house on Banks Street and all the little things she had collected in life. Her father's pipe. Her mother's wedding dress. Her refrigerator magnets. She wondered if her son, a writer of sorts who lived in the northern California redwood-and-wine country, even knew about the hurricane. She wondered how her students in the Advanced English class at Delgado College, whom she had taught for just one week before the storm hit, had made out. She wondered, she wondered . . . She heard some rustling about an aisle or two over and feared it might be rats. Since she couldn't sleep anyway, she finally mustered her nerve and got out of her cot to investigate.

She caught Gastro in the act of rifling through some cardboard containers.

"What's going on?" she asked, and he jumped about a foot.

"I'm, uh, just getting some writing stuff," he said, jamming things into his pockets.

Hope got closer and took a better look. It seemed to her that the open boxes contained calculators and electronic gear.

"I just wanted some paper," Gastro explained, displaying a yellow pad and a handful of pens.

"What are you writing?" she asked.

"Oh, you know, I keep a journal, poetry, stuff like that."

"Really? I'd like to read some, if you ever want me to. I teach students your age."

"Yeah? Well, nobody reads my stuff. So good night, lady." Gastro melted back into the shadows.

Hope shrugged. This hurricane had turned everything upside down. Who knew what belonged to anybody anymore. Maybe we all just had to take what we needed to get through. Suddenly tired, she went back to bed.

16

OVER THE WEEKEND THE RADIO REPORTED THAT THE CITY had reached equilibrium with the lake. The bathtub was full. No more water could get in, unless there was a rain or another powerful storm. Both seemed unlikely because the sky was blue and the forecast was dry. Finally the buses came to the Superdome and the Convention Center, and the haggard refugees were leaving for Houston and points all over America. The Coast Guard and the Air National Guard reported rescuing thousands by airlift and boat. Heartwarming tales of arms opening to the tragic survivors in Salt Lake City, Nashville, Indianapolis, Bismarck, and Tulsa got on the news.

Televised stories of looting had also been broadcast around the globe, or so those gathered around the cooker at the Petrofoods plant learned on WWL radio. They did not yet have any TV reception, though Steve had fashioned an antenna on the tin roof to try to pick up Baton Rouge. They said the New Orleans cops were taking part in the stealing. They said the cops had looked the other way since there was no jail to lock people up in. They said the Wal-Mart on Tchoupitoulas Street, a newly opened megastore battled by preservationists and the small business owners who had previously abounded and added charm to New Orleans, had been cleaned out. Microwaves and toaster-ovens littered Race Street, dropped by people overcome by all the merchandise they had to carry. There was a shoot-out on some bridge Tubby had never heard of between young black men and the police, and the young black men were killed. It was said that news of this battle had cleared the streets of the vultures.

Martial law was imposed in New Orleans and also in Jefferson Parish, where the Petrofoods refuge was located, but this did not deter Tubby and Flowers from making forays into the outside world to learn what was going on. Flowers had his detective badge, of course. Another big asset was Gastro. Using one of the office laptops powered by the generator when Commander Flowers allowed it to be operated, he designed and printed colorful credentials from Governor Kathleen Babineaux Blanco declaring the bearer to be ESSENTIAL HURRICANE RECOVERY PERSONNEL.

There were few official impediments to travel, however. Mostly the problems on the roads were downed trees and building material such as fallen billboards and gas-station canopies. Only occasionally did one encounter a sheriff's deputy, and the officer never took an interest in two white guys in a big truck.

So Tubby and Flowers were able to engage in reconnaissance. They drove around the empty streets of Metairie saying, "Will you look at that!" as they passed extraordinary sights. Such as an apartment building with the front wall sheared away by wind, exposing a dozen rooms, still with furniture inside. Or men loading stuffed deer heads and softball trophies into a pickup from a crushed union hall. Or a McDonald's sign crumpled like an aluminum can. They took Hope on one short trip, to relieve her boredom.

"I guess I was just hoping to see some sign of normalcy," she said, as they passed a boarded-up supermarket.

"There really isn't any." Flowers said. "And there can't be so long as there's a mandatory evacuation. Nobody can come back yet."

Helicopters soared overhead. There were bulldozers and front-end loaders at work clearing the major thoroughfares. They avoided those, not to slow the work, and ventured onto side streets. Here they saw a few humans, a few chain saws getting to work, a few armed residents watching their homes resentfully.

On Sunday afternoon, the lights came back on at Petrofoods. The water heaters worked again. Everybody took a hot shower. The TV still received no channels, but the office air conditioner hummed. Steve asked who wanted to have their cots moved into the office, but nobody jumped at it. In a strange way, they were sad to see the amenities return and life get back to normal. They had begun to enjoy their camp and their unplanned fellowship.

The radio reported that on Labor Day Jefferson Parish would be again open to the public. Access would be restricted to home-owners, and the I-10 was off-limits to all but emergency vehicles. Valero and the other oil refineries in nearby St. Charles Parish were calling workers back. The only thing completely sealed off would be New Orleans. The Petrofoods Company informed Flowers that its administrative staff would be trickling in on Monday and hoped to get back to work on Tuesday.

"So I guess we'll all have to think about . . ." Flowers began.

"Leaving?" Hope completed his thought.

"I'm afraid so."

"I've got a house to look after," Tubby said, "You're all welcome to come with me."

"What's your idea exactly, Tubby?" Flowers asked. "I mean, there's no electricity or water in New Orleans."

"Hell if I know," he said. "Maybe I'll go back and forth from civilization to swamp, but I'm used to this after five months in Bolivia. Anybody who wants to come with me is welcome."

"No plumbing?" Gastro asked. "Sounds like the places I lived in the French Quarter."

"You can come out to Myrtle Grove with me and stay with my auntie. She's got plumbing and she can cook."

Gastro pointed to the dark skin of his forearm and the ring in his nose.

"You don't look no worse than Cousin Billie." Steve said. "She came back that way from Afghanistan."

Gastro shrugged.

"I don't want to put you out," Hope said to Tubby.

"It wouldn't be a problem," he said. "Not for me, at least. You really are welcome to come."

"It would keep me closer to my house," she said. "And maybe I could start cleaning that up."

Tubby said sure.

"I'll have plenty of work to do out here," Flowers said. "But I can help you all get settled in."

So they all made their plans and packed up.

The men loaded a generator, a water purification unit, and about a quarter ton of bottled water and canned goods into the truck. They hooked a trailer on behind and loaded it with twenty plastic four-gallon cans of gasoline and a Port-O-Let toilet, all courtesy of Petrofoods.

"Charge it all to Dubonnet & Associates," Tubby told Flowers.

"I think it will all be covered by their insurance," Flowers said. "If not, you and me can work it out. You wouldn't believe what I'm getting paid for this job."

Tubby was more used to being the giver than the givee. It was a humbling experience, all this kindness, and one of the first nice things to come out of this hurricane. He knew that Flowers's own home, a condo he seldom occupied, was in Algiers, a portion of the city spared by the storm. But the detective knew people—everybody knew people—who had been wiped out.

"Sure," Tubby said. "Let's see if we can smuggle all of this into New Orleans."

They all broke camp. Steve and Gastro drove away in the Nissan Frontier for Myrtle Grove. Tubby, Christine, and Hope waved them good-bye and piled into Flowers's truck. The hound, Rex, hopped into the back seat. It was now legal to be on the streets as far as the New Orleans city line. After that, who knew? They decided to try River Road.

BONNER RIVETTE, after losing his tug-of-war for Christine's right arm, had rolled through the levee grass and then run for the trees. He had sensed rather than heard Flowers's gunshots, and he zigzagged as he went, stumbling through the uneven turf to the wood line, where the Levee Board mowers stopped and wild thickets began. He leaped over a fallen tree into the cover of willows and yaupon. The helicopter was overhead, and Bonner struggled through the brush, getting himself deeper into the woods until the branches overhead concealed him. He was in a veritable hobo haven, that batture land between the river and the levee, often inundated by high water, but which when dry provided a sandy campsite for tramps, degenerates, and lovers. Right now it was dry, for despite the lake's pillaging of New Orleans, the river had never flooded.

Rivette made his way to the shoreline where muddy waves lapped against the sand, and the ground was littered with discarded milk jugs, broken bottles, and coils of yellow and blue poly line. Here was a log where one might watch the sunset, and there were the cold ashes of a tramp's fire. Upstream was a tall metal structure with a green sign on top: PIPELINE CROSSING. DO NOT DREDGE, he read. Downstream was nothing but a woodsy shoreline until the river far below was crossed by electricity transmission towers.

He felt safe. The woods were not unlike those in which he had helped his father cook methamphetamines as a child. The problem, however, was a familiar one, which he also remembered from his childhood. There was nothing to eat. Since it was still broad daylight, he did not fancy returning to civilization, even the post-hurricane remains across the levee. That could wait until after dark. Until then he would bide his time and use his woods skills to build a shelter and try to catch some fish.

The shelter was easy enough. He found a tarp fragment left by a previous hermit and stretched it over some limbs he propped up against a sweet gum tree. He weighted the ends down with driftwood stumps and scoured the leaves from underneath with a piece of two-by-six. That gave him a sandy bedroom.

There was plenty of fishing line tangled in the trees. He made himself a pole from a willow sapling, dug some worms from under a log, and sat down to catch his supper. And he fell asleep.

In his dream he was drowning. Something was holding him under, and he was gulping putrid water. Two arms reached down and rescued him. They belonged to a maid with blonde hair. She was Christine. She held him close and tugged him ashore. On the sand he lay gasping while she cradled his head and kissed him tenderly. Overhead, the helicopters were coming to capture him. They ran through the woods in terror, trying to get away. Branches tore at his face. He looked back and the girl was gone. No matter, because the fight against the enemy-without-a-face was his alone. He hit the ground and began to crawl.

He woke up, laying on the ground, and the pole that had been in his hand was trying to get away. Scrambling in the sand and brush he got a hand on it before it snaked into the water and felt the tug of a powerful creature. He tugged back, worried that his line would come untied or break. And he struggled with his fish until he could see its ugly head under the water. It was a monster cat, as long as his leg, and he was almost unable to bring it ashore. But he worked it out of the shallows until its head and gills were on the beach. The fish heaved and bristled, seeking oxygen it could use, and flapped its great tail in an effort to get submerged again. Bonner found his two-by-six and flailed at the fish until it stopped flopping. The he shoveled it ashore and admired his catch. It would feed a family of four for a week, if he only had a way to cook it.

As dusk fell, he emerged slowly from cover and scouted the levee. He saw no pedestrians, no policemen, no people, just a grassy green slope that curved in both directions as far as the eye could see. Nor were any helicopters immediately overhead. He crept up the embankment to get a view of what lay on the other side. The top was blacktopped, a bike path he deduced from the wind-bent sign a few feet away that explained that bikes must yield to joggers. On the inland side of the levee, fifty yards off, were streets and houses. There was a sign in front of one that read TINY TOM DAY CARE. No traffic was coming from either direction, so he got to his feet and loped to the places once inhabited by humans.

Tiny Tom's was a regular brick ranch house, but the carport was empty. In the backyard, pine trees had blown down and smashed a swing set. The top of a jungle-gym protruded from a pile of green branches. The back door was locked. A decal on the glass advertised a security service. Without hesitation he picked up a fragment of a tree limb and busted through the glass. He waited a second, but he heard no alarm and he saw no excited neighbors. All he detected was the breeze rustling the pine needles. For the first time all day, he smiled. Civilization here was in ruins—all as he had ordained.

The door opened easily when he reached inside and turned the knob. He found himself in a kitchen. It was very quiet. He went from room to room, past piles of toys and a stack of cots where peaceful children had once rested. Satisfied that he had the place to himself, he returned to the kitchen.

Bonner went though the refrigerator and all the cabinets thoroughly, and he came up with some acceptable grub. The ice box stank, of course, since the power had been out for about a week. But he found jars of mustard and pickles and ketchup he thought he could use, and a bag of tiny carrots, and some green olives. He had always liked olives. There was a big tube of bologna, which he also craved, but the end was blue and dripping white jelly so he was forced to leave it behind. Same with a family-sized package of Ball Park Franks.

The cabinets held everything else he needed. There was a frying pan and a pot, used for boiling hot dogs, no doubt. He stuffed a handful of plastic knives, forks, and spoons in his pocket. Here were also jars of peanut butter and jelly, a can of Hershey's chocolate syrup, and a huge box of fruit roll-ups. He was smart enough to run his fingers over the very top shelf, and there it was, a box of kitchen matches, hidden from curious little children. He found salt and pepper shakers and a jug of fruit punch. And there were plastic bags to carry it all in.

Heavily laden, he left the house as he had entered it. The street outside was still dark and deserted. He scrambled across the roadway and up the levee again, bearing his provisions. As he hurried down the other side his foot suddenly got stuck in a hole while the rest of his body kept traveling. He slammed into the hillside, throwing his bags away as he fell. Splayed out on the rough turf, the pain began. It raced up his leg, still pinned in a hole, through his chest to his head and he could not help himself. He yowled. His ankle was on fire.

After a few minutes of twisting in excruciating pain, Bonner collected his wits and eased himself to his knees. He had no idea whether he had broken his ankle or sprained it, but it hurt like hell. He was still twenty yards from the protection of the woods, and his goods were strewn all about him. For the first time, he felt weak and almost wished for the security of his jail cell. All his life, it seemed, he had been alone. Depressing thoughts of self-immolation crossed his mind. Just go up in flames. Funny how it was nature that had tripped him up.

In a few minutes the fire in his ankle subsided and his powers returned. Crawling about, he retrieved as much as he could of his booty. Most important were the matches, and he bared his teeth in a hideous grimace when his hand clutched those again. It was pitch black now, though the sky was full of stars. Gagging from the pain, he hopped, falling sometimes, with his groceries to the trees, and then he used them to support himself, jumping from trunk to trunk, until at last he regained his camp. Cursing himself for not collecting firewood while it was daylight, he lumbered about in the sand, pulling in dry branches and vines to make a pile. He tried one match, then two, then three, before he got it lit. He knew it would be a struggle to keep it going, but he needed the light to eat his peanut butter. The damn fish would have to wait. Even hurricanes had their bad days.

17

THE EVIDENCE OF CIVILIZATION'S COLLAPSE WAS EVERY-
where. Flowers would point out a plywood sign promising
that LOOTERS WILL BE SHOT, and Hope would point out a
convenience store with all the plate glass smashed leaving empty
shelves visible inside. Approaching the parish line they could see
ahead a blockade of police vehicles, lights flashing. Flowers had
his badge ready in his hand.

"Where are those guys from?" Tubby asked. One of the police
cars was maroon with a white roof; the other was white.

"Beats me. Hello, officer," Flowers said through the open
window. He slowed and prepared to stop.

The middle-aged cop waved them through.

"Lexington, Kentucky, Sheriff's Department," Tubby read as
they passed. "They didn't seem too interested in us."

"I guess we don't look like looters," Christine suggested.

"What's a looter look like?"

They crossed the railroad tracks, and they were in. The city
was drab, and trash was strewn everywhere. They stuck to the
levee road, carefully navigating around pieces of tin and roof
shingles, until they reached St. Charles Avenue where it ends at
the river.

"Jeez, look at that!" Streetcar poles were down on the neutral ground. Trees were totally upended, their root balls taller than a bus. Muddy cars sat crookedly on the trolley tracks. The entire way to Tubby's street they spied only one other moving vehicle, a pickup truck coming the other way on the Avenue, its windows smoked.

"I wonder who cleared all the trees off the street?" Tubby asked.

"The Corps of Engineers?" Flowers suggested.

It would be months before they learned that it had been one crazy freelance landscaper with a Bobcat.

"Let's try Nashville Avenue," Flowers said. His tires began crunching over branches when he made his left turn. There was a path of sorts down the middle of the pavement, as if other cars might have passed this way in the week since the hurricane. In a few more blocks they encountered the edge of the flood. Slowly, Flowers maneuvered into the water.

Power lines dangled from the poles.

"I think it's receded some. We might be able to reach my house."

They got close, about a hundred feet short. The water was only a few inches deep, but what stopped the parade was a magnolia tree lying across the street.

Tubby sighed and got out. The tide, now a pale sickly green, wet him to the ankles. The dog splashed happily into the water. Gamely, the three of them unloaded the truck and carried the provisions around the tree and onto Tubby's porch. His whole tree-strewn lawn was now above the water line. The generator was the hardest item to transport since the two men had to keep from stumbling in tandem, but they got it done. Even the gas cans and the water purifier made the trip. Exhausted, they looked at the plastic Port-O-Let.

"Let's just dump it here in the street. I'll figure out how to get it later," Tubby said.

"Nope," Flowers declared. "We can do this. It will float, don't you think?"

It did, a little bit, and eventually they had dragged it where they wanted it.

"Now ain't that beautiful." Flowers admired the bright yellow toilet perched on the Dubonnet porch. "All the privacy a man could want. Just don't fill it up too fast."

Hope groaned and rested on the rail. "I guess this is a good idea," she said.

"At least it's home," Tubby told her. "But if it gets too bad, we can always go out the same way we came in."

"That's what I need to do, folks," Flowers said. "It's time for me to report to work. I'll try to get over here every day or so and check on you."

It took some maneuvering to get the truck turned around and the trailer hitched back up.

Hope and Tubby watched their ship sail away. "Marooned," he said in a low voice. He meant it as a joke, but that was the way they both felt.

All alone in the 'hood, they went back to the porch to unpack. Christine had gone upstairs to try to nap in her old room. She was unusually quiet. Tubby longed for the old racket of jam boxes and televisions he had once complained about. The silence bugged him. There weren't even any squirrels in the trees. And it was hot.

A twenty-five foot tall palm, the pride of Tubby's yard, had fallen and taken with it the power lines running from the pole to his house. They, in turn, had torn his electrical service box, breakers, and meter off the building. He was stumbling around in the jungle of palm fronds and wires trying to figure out how he could attach the generator to his house lights when he was addressed sternly from his front yard.

"Sir!"

The homeowner was so startled that he almost toppled over. Looking through the brush he saw soldiers, M-16s at the ready, black smudges under their eyes like football players. This was it. He was about to be rousted or shot. He clambered out of the palm, wiping his dirty hands on his pants. Rex bounded off the porch swing, the hair on his back bristling.

"Do you live here, sir?" the leader asked. There were four men with him, all dressed in green and black camouflage uniforms and all were strangely suntanned. Tubby noticed another squad watching his arrest from the corner where a stop sign used to be.

"Yes, I do live here. My name is Dubonnet. This is my house. I'm trying to get my electricity working."

"What is the address here, sir?" the leader wanted to know, and Tubby told him. He knew there was a mandatory evacuation order in effect and was deflated, considering all of the work he and Hope had put in readying his house for occupancy.

"There's supposed to be a high school right here, Saint Ing . . ." The soldier couldn't pronounce it.

"Sure," Tubby said. "Saint Ingnatyranius Prep. It's two blocks that way and hang a right."

"Our GPS puts it right here."

"The map's wrong," a soldier behind him observed.

"The map must be wrong," the leader conceded. "What are your plans, sir?" he asked Tubby.

"My plan is to try to get my house operating and to protect my property," he replied staunchly.

"Well, sir," the soldier informed him. "Saint whatever-it-is school will be our base. We will be your force in the neighborhood."

"That's great," Tubby said.

The soldiers turned away and clomped off.

"Where are you guys from?" Tubby called to their backs.

"San Diego. California National Guard," the leader yelled.

"Glad you're here!" Tubby told them. I wish you could have been here a week ago.

He went inside to tell Hope that they had a force in the neighborhood. She was in the back, dragging branches away from the patio doors so that they could be opened. He could see that a rather large wax myrtle from his neighbor's yard had knocked down the fence between them.

"They didn't tell us to leave?" Hope asked, surprised.

"No, they just wanted directions."

"Do you smell smoke?"

"Kind of. I've been smelling something burning for a while."

"Shouldn't we, like, check on it or something?"

"I guess so. I could use a break anyway."

The two of them ventured out onto the street again.

"I think it's coming from that direction," Hope said, and Rex led the way.

The smell grew more obvious as they proceeded, and they had only gone a block when they both exclaimed "Whoa!"

Five houses on the corner were completely gone, burned to the ground. Just brick porch columns and the iron fences around the edge of the properties remained standing. The lots were heaps of smoking rubble.

"It's still burning," Hope said, pointing to a bright red flame dancing three feet into the air above the pile and roughly in the middle of the carnage.

"That could catch the whole neighborhood on fire," Tubby said. "I'll go get the National Guard."

Leaving the woman behind, he jogged the three blocks to St. Ignatyranius Prep. He found the soldiers, including the very one who had spoken to him, sitting on the front steps eating chips. They still had their weapons slung on their shoulders.

"There's a fire," he gasped, almost done in from the exercise. "There's a fire," he repeated, pointing.

The guardsmen took him seriously enough to walk with Tubby back into the neighborhood, but they wouldn't run.

Yes, indeed, there was a fire still smoldering.

The leader went into a private conversation on a walkie-talkie. He frowned at his spectators.

Tubby began to get paranoid. There was, after all, a mandatory evacuation in effect, and he and Hope were not evacuated.

"Let's get back to our house before they run us all out," he said to Hope. "These guys can take care of things, and if we stay here they might arrest us."

"The flame is coming from that gas pipe," she told him.

"Yeah?" Tubby asked. He was impressed by her deduction. "I wonder why they can't just turn it off."

Half an hour later, he saw the National Guard march back past his house, returning to base. Tubby slipped out to reinspect the fire, and nothing had changed. The eternal flame burned brightly. The rubble smoked. The intersection was empty of people.

He decided to try to find where the gas meter was. Perhaps he could turn it off. But most of the places between the sidewalk and the foundation were covered in hot coals, so he did not get very far. Several cars parked beside the building had been incinerated. Beside one of these was a silver puddle shaped somewhat like an electric guitar. He touched it gingerly. Wait, it was melted aluminum. One of the car's sporty wheels. At what temperature does cast aluminum melt, he wondered. A thousand degrees? He took the sculpted guitar home to show off to his new family unit.

Their first night together was a little bit awkward. Christine was unsure what the relationship between her father and Hope was. Tubby tried to make it clear that they were just hurricane friends, and he installed Hope in the guest room. There was a girls' room upstairs for when any of them visited, and Christine staked that out. She even found some of her old things in the closet. The problem of who would cook was solved when Tubby volunteered to heat up the Petrofoods Rice-a-Roni himself on the Coleman propane stove. They ate by lantern light because his first attempts to hook up the generator had been cut short by the National Guard, the fire, and darkness. He suggested a game of Hearts, but the ladies were yawning. Christine took matters into her own hands and went to bed.

"The guest room is made up," he told Hope. "Nobody's slept there since I went down to Bolivia."

"Bolivia? That must have been interesting. Did you just get back?"

"Yes, the day before the hurricane. It seems like a year ago, but it's only been a week."

"Whatever were you doing down there?"

"Just some business," Tubby said vaguely. "Have you ever been to South America?"

"I went to Rio once for Carnival. It was a long time ago when I was single. Now I'm just a school teacher who can't afford to go anywhere."

"But you've obviously had some memorable experiences. Want a drink?"

"Sure," she said. "And then it's off to bed."

"How about some of Flowers's rum? It's ten years old."

She nodded. Tubby brought her a glass with a little warm Coke. She sipped it quietly.

"Lost in thought?" he asked, almost asleep himself. They were sitting in his kitchen on Home Depot stools.

"That man who kidnapped your daughter, what did he look like?" she asked.

"He was tall. He was lean and had a long gaunt face. Of course, he hadn't shaved so he looked like a derelict, except his clothes were new. But they clashed, like Steve Martin or something. His eyes are deep in his head. He had big ears. I'd say he was barely twenty. He looked strong."

"I think I saw that man," she said after a moment. "On the bridge. He took my blanket. Then I think he beat up some man and threw him into the water."

"Then I guess we'd both like to see him brought to justice," Tubby said.

"Justice." She savored the word. "That sounds so complicated. Brought to justice. When our whole world is falling apart. In Biblical days, the bad were just swept away. Temples fell on them. Plagues carried them off."

"I know what you're saying. Only I've been a lawyer for so many years I think about justice . . ."

"You look very tired," Hope told him.

They both fell asleep. Much later, Hope tapped Tubby on the shoulder, and they both dragged off to bed.

18

THE DAYS PASSED. AND LIFE WAS NOT DULL. TUBBY GOT INTO the physical side of cleaning up things. He chainsawed the trees out of the street, and out of his yard, and off of his neighbor's roofs. They made friends with the National Guard and tried their first MREs. "Cajun Style Rice with Beans and Beef Sausage Smoke Flavor Added" wasn't bad. "Chicken Casserole" drew complaints. The only way to make the dry crackers taste good was to coat them with cheese sauce sizzled up in the heating pouch. Hope pointed out that between the pretzels and dip and cheese, they had used up seventy-eight percent of their daily salt intake requirements before even getting to the main course.

Menfolk who had evacuated their families returned one-by-one to see the damage, and they brought care packages of groceries, beer, and soft drinks. When they had more than they could use, Tubby and Hope invited the Guardsmen over for dinner. By now the Californians had left, replaced by Louisiana militia happy to be home from Iraq. A girlfriend of Christine's, Samantha, showed up without any fanfare. She moved into Christine's room and hardly ever came out. The generator worked much of the time, and Tubby got a big security light working that could light up the back yard like a football stadium.

He was actually as happy as he could remember being. The hurricane had given him back a family and a sense of usefulness. True, Christine moped around sometimes. That was natural considering what she'd been through. But the manual labor felt good. It was as though they were all pioneers together. Christine did not speak about her ordeal with Rivette very often, but she pitched in around the house and seemed to be getting okay. She didn't talk as much as she used to—as much as her mother did.

Tubby was bittersweet when Christine announced that she and Samantha wanted to get back to civilization and school. But they were right. Life goes on. So Tubby connived a pass from his neighborhood Guardsmen so he could not only travel out of New Orleans but also get back in. He left Hope in charge of what he called Camp Dubonnet, borrowed a car from Flowers, and drove the girls to Jackson, Mississippi, where his ex-wife was staying with some of her friends. They owned a house in a gated community beside a small private lake. When he got there he joked that the security reminded him of New Orleans, but of course it was far better. The sense of safety in his city was derived solely from the fact that New Orleans was basically deserted of everybody except soldiers and engineers.

On the drive to Jackson the lawyer learned that Samantha had lived after the storm in an apartment over a bar in the French Quarter, sharing the space with the owner. They hid from the looters and police, ate peanut butter and bottles of cherries, bathed in club soda, and used a beer stein for a chamber pot which they emptied out the window into the courtyard. "Just like in the old days," she said, recalling legends of the time when all of the Vieux Carre's waste was deposited into open ditches flushed mainly by rain. Samantha had lived this way for nine days, lasting that long because she and her roommate consumed tubs of warm Bud Lite. But it was so dank and smelled so bad that they finally decided to flee. In the course of their lodging they had lost all romantic interest in one another. On his robin's egg blue Vespa, they snuck out of the Quarter at dawn when they hoped the Guardsmen and looters would all be asleep and took back streets Uptown. With the luck of the young, they reached Camp Dubonnet unmolested. There the boyfriend bade Samantha a hasty farewell and set off for a better place in Houma. She was grateful to see him leave. All of this was related by Christine, because Samantha didn't want to speak about it.

Though she had cleaned up for the trip north to Mississippi, Samantha was obviously subdued and confused by her recent ordeal. The raucous welcome the party received upon landing at the lake house in Jackson drove her into the bathroom, and Tubby never saw her again on that trip.

It was not just Tubby's ex-wife, Mattie, and his other two daughters who greeted them at the door, it was also Mattie's hosts, two well-heeled, well-lit good-timers in the real estate business, and a half-dozen of their neighbors and friends busy drinking chocolate martinis and grilling enormous pork chops out by the dock. For the first time, Tubby let some of his hurricane intensity go and just allowed himself to be hugged and yakked at by Debbie and Collette. Though the TV in the den was turned to CNN and still carried non-stop Katrina news concerning the future of evacuees in the Houston Astrodome, and the belated plugging of the holes in the New Orleans levees by the Corps of Engineers, there were drinks aplenty and a noisy, affectionate, air conditioned atmosphere that blended perfectly with Tubby's new and euphoric embrace of human fellowship. Their host donned a white yacht-captain's hat and took most of the group out onto his party barge for a swing around the lake.

Tubby stayed behind and found himself talking to an attractive realtor from Ocean Springs who had just that day arrived from the Coast. Her home, set a mile back from the beach on the bay side, had been partially smashed by a tree, while she bravely braced herself against the wind in her second-floor bedroom. After the storm had passed and she was outside assessing the damage, and thanking heaven for her survival, something in the house ignited and the entire structure blazed to the ground in half an hour. Though a couple of weeks had passed, she was still in a mild state of shock and awe, but was drinking Scotch and exhibiting the brave and unflappable character that is bred into some Southern women. Many of her friends had also lost their homes. Why, she had heard, all six federal judges in southern Mississippi had been totally wiped out. Her friend, the Senator, had seen his own house swept away. Maybe it was time for her to just buy a condo. She really didn't need a five-bedroom home. All the children were grown up anyway. Tubby liked her. They flirted. The hurricane was somewhere else.

When the pontoon boat returned and the pork chops were devoured, Tubby left. After-dinner drinks were still being served, and he was offered a couch to sleep on, but it seemed too cozy, with his ex-wife in the guest room. He drove back to the Interstate and inquired at the Holiday Inn Express, the first motel he saw. They were full. So was the Ramada across the street. He had been afraid this would be a problem since the hurricane winds had also plastered Jackson, since gas was hard to come by south of the city, and since recovery workers were hogging all the rooms. But he was lucky at the Hampton Inn. He enjoyed his first good night's sleep since, when? Sometime back in Bolivia, maybe. He woke up in the morning so late that all the sausage and biscuits were gone at the free breakfast buffet in the lobby, and he had to make do with an English muffin and a banana. Carrying them back to his room, he shared an elevator with a guy wearing a FEMA T-shirt. Tubby smiled politely. The government man flinched as if he'd been struck. Tubby made a small pleasantry to reassure him. The lawyer was reaching out and touching everybody. Before Tubby left the world, he loaded up on supplies—frozen steaks and toilet paper and a box of oranges, and a case of wine and everything else he could think of and could pay for with an American Express card. He got all the things that he used to take for granted at his local Winn-Dixie which, sad to say, had been picked to the bones by marauders. He had to wait in line for half an hour at an Exxon station for gas, but the automated pump also obliged him by accepting his credit card. This was great. Where was AMEX going to send the bill? He kept pumping until he had filled up his two red spare containers in the back, and then he stomped on the pedal and rolled on down that Interstate highway pointed south. He raced along with caravans of electric company cherry-pickers from Indiana, military convoys from Michigan, and fire trucks from Ohio. Every last one of them was going eighty miles an hour, and they were en route to rebuild New Orleans. Tubby felt the love. Blasting down the highway he knew he was part of something glorious and big.

BONNER RIVETTE got used to living in the woods, just a convenient hop, skip, and a jump from a dozen blocks of flooded and abandoned houses. They were loaded with food and booze and clothes and he even found a lid of marijuana hidden in a bread box behind a moldy loaf of Arrowhead rye. Of course, he had to slip around patrolling sheriff's cars and, after about a week, soldiers, but he only went out at night, had no vehicle to mark his presence, and took one small load at a time. He was hard to spot. There was no river traffic, so no one noticed him from the water. He did not know it, but because of downstream hurricane silting, the Mississippi River was closed to navigation. He supposed the occasional helicopters overhead or the passing police car on top of the levee might spot his fire back in the brush, but no one ever came to investigate. His ankle healed, and now that his internal energy was building he felt ashamed at the weakness he had formerly displayed. Had he offended the woodland spirits? He meditated about this to re-secure his place among his pantheon. Nevertheless, even with the spirits present, he was lonesome. Camping out was not getting him closer to realizing his yearnings. He hoped to locate the source of Katrina's power. It was almost time for the storm to get busy destroying things again.

One morning while Rivette sat meditating by the river, seeking strength from the wind, he heard an unfamiliar noise through the broken stand of willow trees that sheltered his lean-to. He crept to the edge of the woods to investigate. It was the sound of honking cars. He took a chance and sprinted up to the crest of the levee and saw below him a long line of traffic moving down the river road. Individual vehicles peeled off onto the side streets. He quickly dismissed the idea that this was a manhunt for him. What it was, he realized, was the return of the rightful owners of these houses. Something had happened to allow them to come back to Bonner's world.

This would be the end, he knew, of his wilderness experience. He prepared himself mentally to reengage in his battle with society. It was time for the knight of disruption to return.

He dressed himself for the occasion, in a pair of crisp Dickey work pants he had taken from a laboring man's closet, pressed neatly by some hard-working wife. Bonner also had a stack of clean T-shirts he could carry in a child's school backpack. They advertised everything from the Grand Canyon to Blackmon's Tree Service. He'd found a nice leather shaving kit, loaded with toiletries he could use. He was deficient in, but not without, ID and cash. For the former, he had a Jefferson Parish voter registration which he had found in the drawer of a man's home-office desk. For cash he had a kid's piggy bank. He had found it stuffed with nearly fifty dollars worth of coins and tooth fairy money. He also had some old silver dollars, set in Plexiglas squares, but he recognized these as items more valuable sold than spent. And he had some papers he had taken from Tubby Dubonnet's law office and his handgun.

Bonner carefully washed himself and shampooed his sandy brown hair in a plastic bucket. He shaved himself well.

Everything he needed went into the backpack. Rivette cleaned up his camp by throwing the rest of the stuff he had touched into the river. Pots, pans, the five-gallon paint buckets he had used for chairs, dirty socks, all joined the great flow toward the Gulf of Mexico. He doubted that anyone was actively hunting him for now, what with the overwhelming confusion of the last two weeks, but his mantra was to leave nothing but his footprints behind.

Satisfied that his camp had been erased, he marched over the levee and across the road as if he were a taxpayer, moving quickly to avoid the trucks and trailers of homeowners, men driving, wives looking anxiously out the window, kids fighting in the back, all streaming back to reclaim their simple lives. He hiked up Newman Avenue past houses he had vandalized and nodded to people getting out of their vehicles and assessing their damage for the first time. Out came the ice chests with water and juice. The men were shaking their heads at smashed roofs. The kids were running for the door while mom tried to keep them back.

Jefferson Highway had previously been the outer boundary of his deserted realm. Now it was jammed with cars. The traffic lights still weren't working, so the scene was a little tense. Many of those behind the wheel had been inching along at ten miles an hour all the way from Baton Rouge or wherever they had been jammed in with family or in-laws, or in motel rooms paid for with maxed-out credit cards, and they were beyond ready to get home. No matter that home might be funky with water or exposed to the weather.

All of the stores and gas stations were boarded up or blown empty as Easter eggs, and Bonner wondered if he might have made his move too quickly. It was all very noisy. He felt a little dizzy. This land looked too barren to support him. He successfully crossed three crowded inbound lanes of cars and trucks and sat down on the curb for a few minutes, considering his next step.

He was in front of a gas station. Its canopy had fallen down and knocked over the pumps. He took a package of hard candies out of his pack and ate a few, enjoying the cherry-red ones best, while he watched the cars bump along. He noticed a man working his way down the grassy median between the two halves of the roadway, sticking signs into the ground. They were small, chessboard-sized, affixed onto wire stands, and the man was putting one in about every ten feet. He had a big stack of them, and he had to keep going back to his car for more.

The signs said, HOUSE GUTTING, followed by a telephone number.

Bonner sensed an opportunity and walked over to see what the man was doing. "You need any help, mister?" he asked.

The man was middle-aged, with a large belly, a big mustache, and hair parted down the middle. He straightened up.

"You want to gut houses?" he asked.

"What's that mean?" Bonner was curious.

"That's what you call stripping out all the stuff that got wet. The moldy sheetrock, the furniture, the floors, whatever got flooded."

"What's it pay?" Bonner asked.

"Six fifty an hour, all cash," the man told him, ready to haggle for more.

"That'll work," Bonner said. "For starters."

"You're hired. You wanna begin now?"

"Sure."

"Okay. Grab you some of them signs."

So Bonner had a legitimate job. After putting up all the signs he had to tell the man he had no place to stay, and he saw a flash of doubt cross his employer's face.

"My apartment's trashed," he explained.

"I got a garage you can sleep in. It ain't fancy, and you wouldn't have it to yourself. I got some other guys sleeping in there, plus my dogs, and my wife also has her washing machine in it. How long you need a place?"

"I don't know."

"Well, okay. Let's see how it works." The boss was flexible. "I got some more signs to put up around the neighborhood. Then I'll get you on the job."

This arrangement suited Bonner Rivette just fine.

19

GASTRO HAD BEEN ACCEPTED BY STEVE'S FAMILY AT THEIR compound of Jim Walter homes and house trailers south of Myrtle Grove, where their backyard was basically the Gulf of Mexico. And Gastro, since he was a free-thinker and had a literary bent, readily accepted the Oubres, who in better days had survived by catching shrimp and selling magazine subscriptions. Thirteen Oubres and seven of their dogs were in residence upon the three-acre lot, separated from Highway 23 by a fringe of orange trees. Most of them expected to be there only temporarily, until they could get back to see what was left of their estates further south in Port Sulfur, Empire, and Venice, areas so wasted by the hurricane that they had been cordoned off by the military.

Miraculously, no one in the family had died, though Cousin Charles described being blown a mile back into the swamp. His wife had figured he was gone for good until he walked back two days later with most of his hair missing.

None of the Oubres currently had a job, so they had plenty of time to cook, and play cards, and tell stories, and eat and drink. Gastro got to try out shrimp gumbo "with mama's belt," blackened shrimp, "shrimp with lotsa garlic," and shrimp boudin, since the deep-freeze had to be emptied out.

There was nothing around to steal, Gastro noted, except for the family's plentiful guns which he did not really know how to use. Truth was, he didn't want to take anything that belonged to the Oubres. Their mutual affection toward each other and their kindness toward him were all new to him, compared to the two families he had known. There was his own back in Montgomery, featuring Dad the butt-kicker, and there was his street clan, where even his friends didn't think twice about shafting each other. Gastro was tempted to try to do something nice for the Oubres, but he didn't know what that would be. He didn't have much experience being nice.

He took a walk "through the country" with Steve one afternoon for the fresh air and to get a little high.

"Cause no one ain't gonna test us right now, bro," Steve said.

"You've been tested? I never have," Gastro boasted.

"Sure. I had a permit to carry a gun in Jefferson Parish, and you got to get tested there. Not here, of course. You don't get that too bad in Plaquemines Parish unless you work for the tow boat company or offshore. But we've always had our own boats and did anything we want so long as we can net the shrimp."

"What's with that now?" Gastro was enjoying the calm of the open space back by the levee, where the land met Barataria Bay. There were even a few cows grazing in the sparse grass.

"They say the shrimp is very plentiful now. The hurricane worked the water around good, and the shrimp got lots of what they like to eat. Only we got no boats to catch them with. Everybody's boat is smashed up or way up on dry ground. Who knows when we'll get all that straightened out."

Newly returned seagulls were sprinkled like Fourth of July

sparklers in the wide blue sky, turned into silver by the bright sun.

"Your family," Gastro said haltingly. "They're nice."

Steve laughed.

"They think they're pretty tough. They don't know about being nice."

"Okay, whatever. But I think they're, like, good."

"They're okay," Steve agreed.

Gastro was still thinking about what he might do to benefit the Oubres. "Maybe," he said, "if we go up to New Orleans, I could score some dope and make some money, and it might help." He was looking into the muddy black earth when he said those words.

"I don't know about that," Steve said. "I might still get called back to work for Mr. Flowers. I wouldn't want to mess that up."

They walked on a little further.

"Right there's where the levee broke," Steve said, explaining the mud flat spreading out before them.

There was an old black man sitting on the levee and watching the birds overhead. He had on dirty khaki pants and torn sneakers, and he had a brown paper bag with a bottle in it between his knees.

"Hello, Mr. Plauche," Steve said cordially.

Mr. Plauche invited them closer with a wave of his hand. Steve introduced his friend.

"It's a good day for thinking," Mr. Plauche said.

"We're mostly just walking around," Steve replied.

"I've been thinking about the past," Mr. Plauche said. "The hurricane stirred that up. You need to go back and remember sometimes."

"Yes, sir. I'm sure that's true," Steve said. He ran his fingers through his red hair and looked up at the sky.

"You see that there?" Mr. Plauche indicated a crooked fruit tree growing out of the base of the levee quite close to the gorge the storm surge had carved out. Now it was almost dry.

"Right there used to be a Negro cemetery. Right under that levee. I'd say a hundred people was buried in there."

"Is that a fact? What happened to all of them?"

"Some of their bones has washed away I expect," Mr. Plauche said. He looked into the bottle that was inside the brown paper bag, but he didn't take a sip. "Some of them is probably there right now. And I think that's why the levee broke here."

"Because they built the levee on a graveyard? You mean a curse?" Steve wasn't really humoring the man—he respected curses.

"Yes, a curse. That graveyard and the church what used to be here was stolen, don't you see, from the people who lived here. It was stolen by the Ortegas when they changed all of the land records and claimed this land for themselves so they could sell it to the government."

"I always heard they stole it."

"They sure did steal it! The sheriffs moved the colored people out, and they didn't get anything for their land. And the government bulldozed that church and the cemetery and the people's houses and built that levee right there."

"Maybe it really was a curse then," Gastro said, following the story.

"Sure it was. And more than that. It was weak soil. There was graves and bodies all up under in there. Of course the levee couldn't stand. It just had to wash out where all those old graves were."

They all studied the crater solemnly.

"Yep, right there's where they were," Mr. Plauche said.

TUBBY'S WARM GLOW from his Jackson vacation lasted for about two days. He made it back to his house without too much trouble. Of course, it took four hours to drive from Hammond to New Orleans because of all the people trying to return to their homes in the adjoining parishes and because of all the military convoys. He had to wait in the traffic like everybody else, but when he got back to the city there was only him and the roadblock at River Road to contend with. Alert National Guardsmen were checking everybody's identification, and turning most of the people around.

When it came his turn, Tubby showed his National Guard pass to the military and tried to look like a first responder. The nineteen-year-old soldier, rifle slung over his shoulder, handed the paper back and waved him through.

A little bit of progress was apparent in that some chain saws were at work opening up St. Charles Avenue. Tubby drove to his house and found that Hope had cleared his front yard and packed about ten black garbage bags full of branches. The tree was still there, but the lawn was now visible under the trunk. In fact, she was working there when he arrived, sweating, heavy breasts heaving, in one of his ERACISM T-shirts, working a pair of loppers. She brushed her hair back with her hand when he drove up, and smiled.

Tubby got out of the truck and hugged her. It was an instinctive thing to do. These days he wanted to hug everybody, and her earthy fragrance suited his back-from-the-road tiredness very well.

"I brought you a present," he said, and got the case of wine out of the truck.

"Oh. You've been shopping," she said happily.

"The best of Wal-Mart," he said. "And here's the other stuff you ordered." He handed her a plastic bag full of feminine supplies.

"Why, thank you, sir," she said demurely.

It was almost like they were married, but without the sex. Or, as Tubby remembered the last part of his marriage, it was almost like they were married.

That night he cooked Wal-Mart T-bone steaks on the grill. Instead of charcoal, he used pecan branches from one of the fallen trees down the block. He and Hope powered up the radio, and, after tiring of the Katrina news on United Radio, found a country music station out of Shreveport. They drank some Wal-Mart California chardonnay, and listened to the flushed-quail sound of the occasional helicopter, red lights blinking, zipping overhead.

There were no mosquitoes, which was unnatural because it was very warm. The diners moved as little as possible to avoid overheating on the sultry night.

"I just heard a cricket," Tubby said.

She listened. There it came again. The meek return of nature, to a habitat that had been very unfriendly of late.

"The first critter to return," she said. "It must be a little loony."

"I imagine its friends will be along in a day or two," Tubby said. He took a nip and looked up at the stars.

"I can't remember ever seeing the Big Dipper before, not from here," he said.

"Which one is it?"

"That one." He pointed. "Here, I'll show it to you."

He knelt beside her, reclined in the wrought-iron arm chair, and guided her finger toward the North Star.

"See, follow that one up this way," He raised her hand high above with his own, and suddenly had to bend over and kiss her.

"Umm," she coughed. "The wine went down wrong. Wait, don't stop."

She put her hand on the back of Tubby's head and pulled it down to hers.

"How romantic can this be," she said, coming up for air. "Two flood victims."

"Two flood victims all alone in a formerly grand but now empty city."

"Cast adrift."

"And only themselves. No one else around."

20

So, TUBBY'S FIRST NIGHT BACK WAS GREAT.

But after that, it suddenly wasn't so good anymore. Tubby could not have explained why this happened, but his Katrina-world turned gloomy. It could have been Christine's departure, the unfinished business with Bonner Rivette, or perhaps the oppressiveness of the mess everywhere, but the zing went away.

Hope looked beautiful to him each morning, but he didn't deserve her. New Orleans was a wreck. He had no right to personal happiness. The hurricane was still everywhere he looked.

It didn't take long for Hope to notice the change. Instead of tickling her awake he was getting up by himself at four o'clock in the morning and sitting on the front porch. Left alone, he might sit there till noon.

"You don't want to clean up the street anymore?" she asked.

"They're not even giving us electricity or water," he complained. "I'd like to know where all those power company guys from Ohio went."

"It's coming," she promised. "Be patient."

"This is going to take years to fix," he said.

"We've got years," she said.

"Just think of all the work," he said.

Tubby grew a beard and began to forget what it was like to tie a tie. He learned that the courthouses were re-opening fifty miles away in a town called Gonzales, since everything in New Orleans had been flooded, but why did he need a courthouse? No clients were calling. Or if they were, they were calling his old office, where the phones had been shut off and much of the glass had been replaced by plywood.

The mayor proclaimed that people in his zip code could come back, and some—mostly men—started to. They brought in more chain saws and generators and set about trying to find electricians to turn the power back on. Even this didn't cheer Tubby. A lot of these men had actual jobs.

He saw the signs on the St. Charles Avenue neutral ground advertising law practices opening up, but his own building was still locked, and his doorbell wasn't ringing.

He began to brood and became unhappy if he had to be around anyone.

After a week of this Hope told him that it was all well and good having a man in her life after some time without, but she was too old to have another sulking teenager. Displaying the survival skills a great many people seemed suddenly to have found since the storm, she got on Tubby's phone and tracked down an old neighbor of hers and together they hatched a plan to share a guest house owned by a friend of another friend in Algiers while someone's son-in-law, a contractor, could be persuaded to go in and fix up one of their Mid-City houses. The plan was long and involved, and based on optimism, the goodness of the government, and a supply of city utilities not yet in existence, but Hope said she was leaving. "To get my life back together."

"And honey-bunch," she said, kissing Tubby tenderly on the forehead, "we can try this again some other time when things get back to normal."

Tubby watched her leave, driving away in the truck of whosever son-in-law that was, and he wondered what he was going to do. At least Rex had stuck with him. One more mouth to feed. The dog yawned at him.

Then began the really bad days, while parts of the city came back to life.

He even got in a fight with Flowers. The detective showed up unannounced in his big truck, radiating purpose and good health, and Tubby asked where he'd been so long.

"Working across the river, boss," Flowers replied, a little startled at the tone. "How've you been making it?"

"Everything is magnificent." Tubby ran his fingers through his beard. "Absolutely magnificent. Did you just come to visit?"

"Uh, I'm going downtown to meet with Homeland Security about a job. So I stopped by. Do you need any help around here?"

"Sure, you can help me wash the dishes."

"That's not a problem."

"I was just joking. No, I don't really want any help."

"I'd be glad to," Flowers said.

"I don't need any help!" Tubby shouted.

The conversation was flat after that, and it didn't last long. Flowers slapped him on the shoulder and drove away.

Tubby wondered what his own life would be like in the future. What kind of life did this poor spent city now have to offer him?

On Magazine Street, things were straightened out enough so that he could reclaim his car.

"You kind of screwed me up," he told his mechanic, "blocking my car in like that."

"We had no idea there would be such a storm, Mr. Dubonnet, and we were very busy on the day we left."

Tubby wasn't mollified, but he paid his bill. He didn't say another word.

"I wonder what his problem is?" the mechanic said to his greasy cat when his customer drove off.

With his car, Tubby could cruise downtown and see shopkeepers cleaning out their stores. "We're Open" signs were sprouting from all the bistros. In the Central Business District, though his own building was still closed, he actually saw men in suits on Canal Street. He hid from them, feeling out of place in his dirty jeans and unclipped hair.

Further on he drove, and the streets were blocked with refuse. Tubby was more comfortable in the wreckage. He heard that the I-10 was open so he drove out to New Orleans East, a sprawling neighborhood of ranch-style homes spanning four highway interchanges.

Everything he saw was dead.

All the houses were caked with mud, and all the streets were empty of everything but flooded and abandoned cars. He drove for miles, pausing at intersections guarded by nonfunctional traffic signals, and realized he was the only person for blocks around. Everybody had been carried away, and why would they ever want to return? The water had been ten feet deep in these houses. Thousands and thousands of them. Clients and friends, they were gone.

He drove out St. Claude, and before the soldiers ran him off he spotted Fats Domino's house, bleak as all the rest. All caked with mud. Coming back into the city on Ramparts Street, all the night clubs he passed were shuttered. The buildings were empty. All the stores were wide-open and stripped.

Just miles and miles of mess.

He took to drinking more than he should, but he did, when invited, accept invitations from other men in his neighborhood to grill steaks in the yard. They would all laugh and drink and eat, and go home to houses without women and children. Maybe the families would come back in January, when the schools would be open again.

Tubby got good at using his cell phone. He started to call his daughters every other day. He called people he hadn't seen for years. An Office Depot opened, and he charged a laptop computer. It was wireless. He learned that the CC's Coffee House at Jefferson and Magazine was wired, and even after the shop closed every afternoon at 3 o'clock, because of a shortage of help, he and a dozen others crowded around outside. Tubby learned how to receive and send e-mails. He grew to love the EarthLink girl, café-au-lait, smiling at her screen. But he was pissed.

He began telling everyone he could find in the web world what New Orleans was like, what the hurricane had been like.

Many of these people, he could tell, had actually forgotten about Katrina and were instead thinking about nonsensical events like Thanksgiving. Didn't they know what it was like here?

No, they actually didn't.

Didn't they know that three hundred thousand people had left a great American city, and they couldn't come back because there was no electricity?

No, they didn't.

Didn't he know who was in the World Series? That a Supreme Court Justice had died? That there were suicide bombings every day in Iraq? That there had been an earthquake in Pakistan? That Christmas was coming?

No, he didn't. What did any of that have to do with Katrina? Not one damn thing!

Tubby got fed up with these so-called old friends who just didn't get it.

He got fed up with the government, which just didn't get it.

Massive federal response? Where are the FEMA trailers? Where's the trash man? Where is the goddamned power company?

Where's my insurance adjuster?

Where's the twenty-second roofing contractor who said he'd be out to give me an estimate?

He knew he was leaving the atmosphere. He knew he was drinking too much. He wondered what was going to become of himself.

Gastro and Steve showed up in the dented Nissan and caught Tubby pouring bourbon at eleven in the morning.

"We brought you some jambalaya my mama made," Steve said.

Tubby took the weighty Tupperware container. "This will last me a week," he said. "Thanks."

"Are you all alone?" Gastro asked.

"Yep. Hope moved out. Christine's up in Mississippi. All I got left is Rex."

The sleeping dog heard his name and slapped his tail on the floor.

"Your world is going to rise again, Mr. Dubonnet," Gastro told him. The words surprised even him.

"What's that?"

"Your world. It's going to rise again, Mr. Dubonnet. It's going to get better for you." Gastro didn't quite know what he was saying. But he was trying out a new personality, a positive personality.

"Is that what you believe, Sid?" Tubby asked skeptically.

"That's what I'm learning." Gastro made a rare smile. "There's a lot of human energy coming into focus, right here in New Orleans. I can feel it."

"You know, kid," Tubby said, "I'm not ready to hear that right now."

And they were like kids visiting an old cranky uncle, and they left as soon as they could.

Tubby stared in the mirror and tried to recall that he was a responsible man. He had shouldered the problems of his clients and argued their cases before powerful courts. He had raised a family, and he had paid tuition for private schools. Thank God they were all closed now, since he was nearly broke. It was hard to know exactly what he had since the banks were closed and there was no mail delivery. He had paid his bills for most of his life. Now his mortgage company had given him, and thousands of others, a grace period, and the bill collectors couldn't find him. In a way, he told himself, he shouldn't complain. He should be enjoying this break. But his sunken eyes stared back at him sadly, and the creases under his cheeks made a frown. How could he enjoy himself? He didn't have a job.

He thought maybe he could hustle the kind of legal business friends of judges typically got—such as being appointed lawyer for someone who couldn't be located, or curator for someone's property. Tubby had a friend who was a judge.

Earlier he had saved a newspaper article reporting that the Orleans Parish Civil District Court had rented space in a strip mall in Gonzales, Louisiana, fifty miles away. He tried for two days to get someone to answer the phone at the number listed in the paper, and all he got was a busy signal. So he made the drive. He even put on a suit.

Sure enough, in what might once have been a row of crummy storefronts he found the "courthouse." "Division T" was a group of desks cordoned off by filing cabinets where sporting goods might once have been sold. At one of the desks was somebody he knew, Mrs. Evans, the judge's long-time clerk.

"Hello, darlin'," he said, as if he were the same old confident Tubby. "Whatcha doin' way out here in the country?"

She peered at him over her glasses. "Can I help you?" she asked.

"I'm looking for the judge. Don't you know who I am? Tubby Dubonnet."

"Oh, Mr. Dubonnet. I didn't recognize you with the beard. Isn't this something?" She spread her arms to take in the whole situation.

"It doesn't look that bad," he said. "Where do y'all eat lunch?"

"We pretty much have to bring it with us. There's nothing around here but the RaceTrac gas station, and they mostly have chips. We do have a microwave, though."

"Is there anything that looks like a courtroom around here?"

"Yes," she said proudly. "The judges take turns. It's next door, if you want to see it. There haven't been that many hearings though."

"How about the judge, is he around?"

Her eyes fell.

"No, he's not in today."

"Is he okay?" Tubby was alarmed. "When will he be in?"

"Well, Mr. Dubonnet. You know the judge lost his house in Gentilly."

"No, I didn't realize. Where is he?"

"He hasn't called me today." She was being evasive. "You know he and Mrs. Hughes went to the Bahamas for a few days."

"I've been completely out of touch. Are they still there?"

"Well," she paused again, "Mrs. Hughes is. She's not ready to come back quite yet. And I don't blame her. The judge has been staying in an apartment in Baton Rouge."

"Does he keep regular office hours?"

"Not exactly. But I am here every day."

"I need to see him. Can you give me his phone number?"

"I don't think he has a phone," she said.

That was odd, for a man who had shown up on time for court for twenty years.

"How about an address?"

"He said, not ..." She thought about it. "Mr. Dubonnet, I think it might be good if you went to see him. He's had a hard time." She opened her desk drawer and found a slip of paper and a pencil. She jotted down "4401 Lime Street, Apartment 922," and handed it to Tubby with a worried look on her face.

"Of course, I'll pay him a call," Tubby said. "I don't have anything better to do."

Baton Rouge was just another twenty minutes up the highway. Tubby had no idea where Lime Street was, but he kept asking directions and eventually found a block of two-story apartment buildings arranged around swimming pools, with a few green trees installed here and there to break up the monotony. It was the kind of place Tubby always thought of as "singles apartments."

He figured out how the complex was arranged and located Building "9." Apartment "22" was an inside apartment on the second floor. He took the elevator and walked down a long hall. The door was open. Two maids were working inside.

Tubby tapped on the wall. "Is Mr. Hughes here?" he asked.

"Not right now," one of the maids said.

Tubby could see a pile of green law books piled in the corner of the room. There was a bar set up under the window.

"Did he say where he was going?" Tubby asked.

"Judge Hughes don't say much," the maid said. "But he left here in his bathing suit, so he may be outside by the pool."

Tubby retraced his steps and located the swimming pool on the other side of the building.

There was a figure covered in a white towel on a reclining chair, shielded from the sun by an orange umbrella, and the lump was big enough to be the eminent jurist.

Tubby approached and recognized the head poked out of the towel, though its brow was cooled by a moist washcloth and the eyes were shaded behind sunglasses.

"Morning, Judge," he said pleasantly.

"Uh," the body grunted, and the head tilted slightly in Tubby's direction. "Why, Brother Dubonnet. Pull up a chair. Approach the bench," the judge said with more resignation than excitement.

Tubby found a dry one and sat beside his friend.

"So, howya doin', Al?" he asked.

"Just about like everybody else. Gettin' by. What brings you up here?"

"I came to see you."

"I'm a sight to see, aren't I?" He removed the washcloth. His brown face looked like melting chocolate in the sun. He had a sprinkle of black whiskers on his chin. "It's a sad state of affairs," he remarked.

"What is?"

"Being here instead of up where the scales of justice are at my right hand."

"This is not so bad, is it?"

"No, it's not so bad," the judge agreed. "When we were in law school together we would have thought this was heaven. You want a beer or anything?" He indicated a portable ice chest by his feet.

"No, no, I'm fine," Tubby said. "I thought your drink was Scotch."

"Only after hours," the judge said.

"I see."

"This is daylight, the time of day when I work. I'm drawing a check after all."

"Is that a fact?"

Judge Hughes tapped his sunglasses down his nose and raised his eyebrows at Tubby.

"Of course I get paid," he said. "I'm a state elected official. But I don't earn my money. I don't have any cases. What's with the beard?"

"Just something I'm trying out. I've got time on my hands." As if that explained it.

"How'd you make out in the storm?"

"Not too bad. Just some wind and a little flood. Not like some. I heard your house took a hit."

"Everything's gone," Hughes said sadly. "All the stuff we had after twenty-five years of marriage. The photographs, the personal things you save, the girls' band uniforms, all that stuff . . ." His voice trailed off.

"I'm sorry to hear it. Olivia must be taking it hard."

"Yes, she is. She definitely is. She's only been to the house once. She took one look and says she won't go back there again."

"I heard she's in the Bahamas."

"That's correct, and in the Bahamas she will stay, until her credit cards run out."

"So how is it here? You got an apartment I see."

"It ain't so bad, old friend, but I've got to say I'm a little depressed about the whole thing."

"Well, me too."

They sat together in silence. The umbrella flapped in a little breeze. Tubby's guiding principle in the practice of law had been, "Never screw a client. Never lie to the judge." He wondered what he ought to say to this one.

"Maybe I'll have a beer," Tubby said.

"You do that," the judge said. "I'm going to go to sleep."

21

Bonner Rivette loved his new job. It provided him with an opportunity to see what his sister, Katrina the whirlwind, had caused and to pick through the decay.

His roommates in the garage were three cousins from Nicaragua, and they tried English with big apologetic grins, managing to ask "How's it going?" and "You like to eat?" They all camped out on cardboard and blanket rolls on the concrete slab floor stained with oil. They had a refrigerator and an electric stove. The walls were full of lawn tools and ladders. A metal folding table served both for their meals and the Nicaraguans' games of cards, which Bonner wasn't interested in. What he did like was that his roommates had shoeboxes full of religious statuary and icons, bleeding Jesuses and plastic cards with stern women's faces portrayed on them, the backs carrying frightening religious messages in Spanish. They took these out every day after work, displayed them on the table, and had prayer sessions. Rivette took part, having no idea what the Latinos were saying but fancying that they were worshipping him. He at least grasped the significance of their devotion to blood, suffering, and terrible sanctions.

Rivette would retire early to read the old magazines his employer stacked in the garage, mostly *Popular Mechanics, Bow*

Hunting, and the *NRA News.* He picked up some new ideas about weaponry, trapping, and how to make effective gun silencers from beer cans. He called his roommates "The Mexicans," and he would pretend to fall asleep in a dark side of the garage while they kept playing their games into the wee hours. But he was actually studying them, memorizing their facial gestures, the way they laughed and ran their grimy hands through their hair when agitated. When they threw in their cards and turned off the lights, brushing teeth and saying good night to each other as they got into their bedrolls, he would stay awake listening, hearing how their breathing and coughing slowed, until they slept. Other people were interesting, but he refused to like them.

He could hear the owner's cat mewing outside the building, and her fury and excitement when she pounced at the mice scampering about appealed to Rivette more. He made sure everyone was fast asleep before he allowed himself to relax and enjoy private thoughts of mayhem, just as he had always done in his jail cells.

In the morning the owner banged open the door and summoned everyone to work. Bonner was always awake already. He generally arose in the last hour of darkness and sat at the table, watching the Mexicans snore, and he sometimes fixed himself a cup of instant coffee. In those quiet moments he often thought about Christine Dubonnet, and he became convinced that she could learn to love and understand him. He imagined apocalyptic scenes he might create, and she was there, swinging a sword beside him. In some scenarios they both died, hands and hearts joined.

But when their employer announced daylight, and the Mexicans got out of bed insulting each other and pissing loudly into the toilet, Bonner was content to stop thinking and journey forth into the moonscape where they would spend their day.

They were carted by pickup truck to the job, someone's flooded home or business, and set to work tearing out all the moldy slimy glop and residue of human existence and dragging it to the street. It smelled bad. It was foul beyond belief. Water, left in a house for a week or two, created a smell worse than the decaying corpse Bonner had once discovered in his father's tool shed. It smelled worse than the effluent through which Rivette had swum when he escaped the New Orleans jail. But it didn't bother him, because it was the evidence of the storm's potent vengeance upon the people who lived in little boxes who Bonner hated with a passion. He equated the storm's power with his own and its smells with virtue.

The Mexicans didn't complain about the work either and just joked and shouted at each other all day. Their laughter bounced off the purple and yellow fungal walls when they turned up something suggestive, like a pack of condoms or a woman's underwear or a girlie magazine. They went positively bonkers over a black rubber dildo that came up from the mud.

Bonner didn't know what it was, and he feared touching something so alien and mystical. When one of his co-workers waved it in front of his face, jabbering incoherently, Rivette knocked it away and barked at the man like a dog. The Mexican backed up, then shrugged in resignation and pitched the toy into the rubble.

Everything they handled went to the street. Wheelbarrows full, until the mountain outside on the curb was the length of the property and as high as the grossness could be thrown.

Every other day the owner paid them in cash. The Mexicans were reluctant to go anywhere to spend their money, and Bonner suspected they were no more legal than he was. So they made shopping lists for the owner's sister, who would go and buy them supplies at Sam's Club on Airline Highway.

Bonner usually ordered the same thing. Cheerios and milk

and Campbell's Chicken Noodle Soup—comfort food.

The owner was extremely successful in lining up jobs. There was no end to the work. He was very happy and promised all of his men a raise. He brought the Mexicans a bottle of Tequila and gave Rivette a fifth of Jack Daniels.

It was a mistake. The party that night in the garage got out of hand. The Mexicans forgot about their suppers in the microwave and burned their frozen El Paso Quesedillas and Bean Dip platters from Sam's Club. They didn't care, but whooped at the smoke pouring out of the unit and shoved each other merrily. They jostled Bonner, who was trying to stir his soup over an electric hot plate, and made him spill his saucepan. While he stared in fury at his dinner sizzling on the burner, the fools grabbed a garden rake and a shovel off the pegboard wall and dueled among themselves, circling around a lawn mower jabbing and feinting. Bonner, his hands wet with noodles, lost his temper. He took up a machete and waded into the game.

He caught one of the Mexicans on the shoulder, slicing it like a watermelon, and the man howled in agony. That ended the fun part of the party. As they retreated before him, Bonner swung his machete in great arcs, intent on decapitating all three of them. They were cunning but helpless before his fury and found themselves pinned into a corner, on their knees, one crying in pain as blood soaked his shirt. The others were also crying, from fear. The eldest held up one of his treasures, a plaster Christ wired to a wooden cross. The Jesus perpetually writhed in agony and blood flowed from his lips. Sharp thorns circled his head, and his eyes were turned upward, searching for relief.

Those eyes stared at Bonner, and he was moved. Throwing aside his machete, he knelt and begged the terrified Mexicans and their insensible Jesus for forgiveness. Then he rose and ran from the building and fell upon the bed of his employer's pickup truck out in the driveway and prostrated himself in his grief. He felt a calling to serve the Lord.

The emotions passed quickly, however. He regained his composure, as he had always managed to do. It was the Lord who should serve him. Gaining his feet, he straightened his dirty work clothes and marched back into the garage.

The Mexicans were ready for him this time. One had the machete he had tossed aside, and the other had acquired an axe from the wall.

"Just here to get my stuff, hombres," Bonner said, smiling.

They accepted that as an invitation to battle. When they tried to encircle him, he overturned the kitchen table and the box with all the saints inside. They pounced, and Bonner defended himself with vigor and great noise, and in a matter of minutes the owner had arrived, threatening to call the police, while Bonner and the Mexicans wrecked the room.

When it was over, the police did come. The owner hid two of his Mexicans under his wife's bed. The other, bleeding profusely, was locked inside a bathroom where he wouldn't stain the carpets until the coast was clear. He sat on the toilet, dribbling hydrogen peroxide into his wound. The officers interrogated the homeowner about all the mess and the blood in the garage, but he explained that there had been a little fight over a poker game. Everybody had split. No harm, no foul.

Bonner Rivette, knapsack full of clothes and some cash in one hand, had vaulted over the back fence and run through the neighbor's yard into the next block. He was on his own in the world again.

The City of New Orleans had filled up with professional debris-removers from Texas. They were mostly young guys, happy to be away from home and making good money courtesy of FEMA. They spent their days driving Bobcats and lifting the piles of debris into big dump trucks, and they got to wear orange vests. They could see that the work before them was extensive. In fact, it might last for years.

Four of them had gathered for lunch at the Daiquiri Shop at Riverbend where roast beef sandwiches had always been the house specialty at $2.95. In their honor, the price had gone up to five bucks.

"That's the kind of girl I always wanted," one of the workers remarked to his friends, referring to the barmaid who was squirting Kahlua icees into twenty-ounce plastic cups. "If she had any more tattoos I couldn't resist."

"Here comes one more my style," his buddy said, sipping his Miller Draft.

The men followed his glance to a large black transvestite wearing a sequined vest and cowboy hat who entered the establishment and went straight to the video poker machine.

"Must be the locals returning."

"She's a honey."

"How about that dude?"

They looked out the window.

An Easy Rider look-alike wearing camouflage pants, and a blue and white windbreaker, and an American flag bandana tied around his head was hiking down the neutral ground where the street car had once run.

"Just another local citizen headed off for gainful employment," one of the men joked.

In fact, it was true. Bonner Rivette had decided to claim New Orleans as his own, and he was on his way to apply for work. Folded neatly in his jacket pocket was a leaflet he had torn off a telephone pole seeking "Certified Hazardous Material Clean-Up Workers/Other Positions Also Available." He thought he was the kind of guy who might fit into an "other position."

TUBBY THOUGHT OFTEN about Bonner Rivette. It festered until, one morning looking in the mirror and not liking the care-worn face staring back at him, he resolved to do something about it. He called Flowers, who had landed a contract with Homeland Security doing background checks on the bevy of prospective law enforcers Katrina had brought into the region.

"It's a fantastic deal," Flowers explained. "I've hired people to work the phones and the computers and run checks on people. I'm just the administrator."

"I never really thought of you in that capacity," Tubby told him.

"Actually, most of the administration is done by Eva, my assistant, but it's like everything else, somebody's got to be the boss."

"So you're no longer a private detective?"

"Sure I am. I can do private work. There's just not much of it to do. I think people must be too busy surviving to worry about cheating on their husbands or getting divorced. And you're not giving me any business. None of the lawyers are. Except someone may want to locate a relative. I've had a couple of those with mixed results."

"I want to locate the guy who kidnapped my daughter, the one called Bonner Rivette."

"He's going to be hard to find until he gets arrested again," Flowers said. "I can tell you what I already know about him."

"You already checked him out?"

"Of course. I do that for anybody who shoots at me and molests the daughters of my friends."

"This isn't a joke."

"Sorry, I didn't mean it the way it sounded."

"Because it's not funny."

"Okay. Rivette is a small town boy originally from Cottonport. He has a juvenile record for something I didn't bother trying to dig up. He has plenty of adult stuff that will give you the picture. Assault with intent to kill when he was eighteen. He attacked some poachers in the woods. Charges dropped when witnesses refused to testify. Convicted for burglary of a church when he was nineteen. All it said was he took items valued at more than a thousand dollars. He pled guilty and got probation. By then, I guess, he was getting to be a familiar face to the local cops because he has two or three more arrests right in a row for vagrancy and getting into fights, but no convictions. They were rousting him, but he was smart. Then he hits the big time and stabs his sister. Actually, he's charged with slaughtering the girl's preacher, too, but that gets reduced to second-degree murder, since he killed the only witness except Sis, and she's a nutcase. He caught a break and only got ten years. He must have been up at Angola when he got a retrial, and then he escapes from some little parish jail. That's when our boy gets arrested again in New Orleans. The storm comes along, and he escapes, again."

"That's all very disturbing." Tubby was indeed disturbed. He had a vision now of Rivette as a mad dog.

"Yes. Christine was lucky to get away from him."

"He hasn't turned up since?'

"You mean since he jumped out of my helicopter?"

"Right."

"No, he hasn't turned up, but it won't be long before he gets caught again. He's too bad, or too outrageous, or too crazy. He'll get picked up for something any day now."

"I'd like to be sure of that and find him myself."

"I guess you could go up to Pointe Croupee Parish or Archie and Bunkie where he used to live. Maybe somebody there has seen him. But detective work is very tedious and time-consuming, Tubby."

"I know. I've paid your bills for years."

"Exactly. Do you want me to try to find him for you?"

"No, I've got more time than money these days. What are the chances that the New Orleans police are actively searching for him?"

"No chance at all. Their headquarters got flooded and the police are all living in one of those cruise ships tied up down by the Riverwalk Shopping Center. They say it's because most of the cops lost their homes to the hurricane. I think it's so the brass can keep an eye on them and make sure no more boys in blue desert or go around looting stores. I think they have their hands full."

"Doing what? We haven't had a murder here since Katrina, and hardly any other crime, they say."

"I don't know—investigating themselves, maybe, or setting up road blocks to keep people out of the Ninth Ward or fixing up their own houses. I can tell you the names of the officers who collared Rivette at the Greyhound station though, if you want to go talk to them yourself. It's Johnny Vodka and Frank Daneel."

"Funny names for Irishmen."

"What? Yeah, funny. If you need any help, you know how to reach me."

"Sorry I was such a jerk the last time I saw you," Tubby said.

"I didn't notice," Flowers lied.

22

THE *ECSTASY*'S BERTH ON THE MISSISSIPPI RIVER WHARF downtown had a look of permanence. The ship was almost surrounded on the land side by police and fire department cars and emergency rescue vehicles parked in orderly rows. Trailers functioning as headquarters for FEMA, Homeland Security, firefighters and cops guarded the approaches to the vessel, and electrical, water and sewer lines had been run to these makeshift offices. A companion ship, the *Sensation*, was docked next door. It housed unfortunate municipal employees.

Tubby had to park half a mile away because a debris mountain had appeared on the regular cruise terminal lot. It was full of bedding and garbage and discarded MRE containers and the rest of the stuff scraped out of the nearby Convention Center after they got all the refugees out of the way and off to Houston. Tubby had heard reports of murder and rape during the days of chaos in this building. One of the old pool hustlers who hung out at a bar Tubby had begun to frequent claimed to have personally seen a man shot between the eyes and the corpse of a seven-year-old girl. City officials denied that such events had occurred, and Tubby questioned how the shark, who was admittedly a steady drinker, knew the girl was seven, but his own brief experience at the Convention Center led him to believe that any horror was possible there.

He inquired at the police trailer where he might find a Detective Vodka. After he showed his ID and offered some wisecracks to establish that he was a serious man and a lawyer with information about a case, the desk officer, hair slicked back like a young James Brown, picked up the phone and made a call.

"He's off duty. But they think he's here. Have a seat." The policeman indicated a rusty folding chair. Tubby took it and waited. He and the desk officer were not the only people around. A lady cop was doing her nails, sitting in front of a little table that had an automatic coffee pot on it. If there had been any conversation in the room, the lawyer's arrival had stopped it. The hands on the electric clock on the wall, fifteen minutes slow according to Tubby's cell phone, did not seem to move.

"Pretty busy down here," he said, trying to liven the place up.

"It's always busy," the desk officer said, scratching his ear with a pencil. He didn't catch the humor.

"I guess you'll be looking forward to getting back to your headquarters."

"Yeah, but they don't say when. The old building is full of mold. It's got some issues."

"Do you like it down here?" Tubby asked.

"I don't stay on the ship," the man said. "I got an apartment across the river in Westwego. You like it here, Trylene?"

"It's okay," she said, filing her pinkie. "But the cabins are too small for my style."

The door to the tin can opened.

"Johnny, this man says he has some information for you," the desk officer said, making the introduction.

Tubby stood up. He was a head taller than Vodka, but the

smaller man gave him a good crunch when they shook hands.

"Come on outside. Let's talk," Vodka instructed. He was wearing jeans, running shoes and a red sweatshirt. He had long blond hair, a mustache like a toothbrush, big ears that might have invited ridicule when he was a kid, and he worked out. At least that's what Tubby figured, judging from the bulges under the cop's sweatshirt.

The policeman led them down the steps to someone's car. He sat on the hood. "Whatcha got?" he asked.

"The day before the hurricane you arrested a man at the Greyhound station named Bonner Rivette."

"That's right, I sure did. Me and my partner. He was wanted on escape from Point Croupee Parish."

"You put him in jail?"

"That's it. No telling where he is now. They bused those prisoners all over the state. The whole parish prison flooded, you know."

"They didn't bus him anywhere. He escaped again."

"No shit?" Vodka exclaimed. "I can't believe how dumb they are down at that crazy jail. They couldn't keep a corpse in a meat locker. It's disgusting. How'd he get out?"

"I don't know. They didn't tell you anything about it?"

"I don't think the sheriff even knows what he had for breakfast this morning, much less where the prisoners are. If we go to arrest somebody today we got no place to take them. Might as well shoot them. We either got to let them go or shoot them, simple as that. No jail, capiche? You tell me where Rivette is, I'll go shoot him. Simple as that."

"I don't know where he is. But the day after the storm he broke into my office. Then he got hold of my daughter and beat her up. He could have killed her."

"Is she okay? You're lucky. That guy is a bad actor."

"I understand that. And then he gets me on the phone to come down there, which is at the Place Palais, and . . ." Tubby told the whole story.

"So the last time he was seen was when he jumped out of the helicopter?"

"That's right."

"That was in Jefferson Parish," Vodka said thoughtfully.

"What's that got to do with it?"

"Lots. It's out of my jurisdiction."

"What if he's not still there?"

"He could be anywhere, right?'

"Sure, but can't you send out a bulletin or something so they'll at least be looking for him?"

"That's no problem," Vodka said.

"And he could very easily be in New Orleans."

"Pal, anybody in creation could be here. We got people here from Texas, Ohio, the Carolinas. We got Mexicans and Canadians and Guatemalans and God knows what all. More of 'em come here every day. You been out to City Park?"

Tubby said no.

"You ought to see this. They got that neutral ground on Orleans Avenue full of trucks and tents and guys sleeping in cars. They're clean-up crews and tree-cutters from everyplace you never heard of. They got a whole tent city out there by the stadium, They got campfires, cooking right there in the trees. It's like the Boy Scouts or something."

"Aren't the police checking who these people are?"

Vodka scoffed. "No. Nobody's checking nobody. Anyway, it's FEMA driving this bus. Not us."

"So there's nothing you can do?"

"I can put him on the list. Look, I'd like to see this Rivette guy fry. I got kids myself."

"And that's one reason I think he may be around here."

Vodka lifted his eyebrows.

"My daughter. I think he may come back for her."

Vodka lifted his eyebrows. "Has he tried to make contact?"

"Not to my knowledge, but I saw the guy up close, and just from a few things Christine has told me it's like he wanted to form some kind of mental bond with her."

"Where is your daughter now?" Vodka asked.

"She's safe in Mississippi, but she's got to come back sometime. She's in college here. They're talking about opening up Tulane University in a month or two, and she'll come back for that. Besides, if it's not my daughter, he may find someone else's."

"Sure, I see your point. I'd like to get the guy myself. Just cause I already caught him once, he should stay caught. Like I say, tell me where he is, I'll be glad to put him out of his misery."

"Simple as that," Tubby said.

"Right," the policeman agreed.

BONNER THOUGHT it was all pretty cool. Not only did they give him a job, but they gave him a white jumpsuit made out of some kind of stretchable paper, and a white cap with an elastic band, little white booties to put over his shoes, white gloves, and a high-quality face mask. It wasn't one of those flimsy disposable kind, like his last boss had supplied, but one made of metal and rubber with two circular protuberances filled with cans of crystals that made him look like a beetle when he put it on. In short, he was covered from head to toe, except for his eyes. Nobody would have the slightest idea who he was.

The man at the application center, a table set up outside a high school on Carrollton Avenue, had asked for identification, of course.

"We have to make sure you are a citizen, sir," the man said.

Bonner laughed. "I ain't no Mexican," he said. "Here. This is all I got. The rest was lost in the storm. My house got flooded."

He handed the man a card stating that he was an honorary Orleans Parish deputy sheriff.

"Is that all you have?" the man asked.

"No, I also have this," Bonner handed him a library card.

"Okay, well I guess that will suffice, Mr. Dubonnet. Am I pronouncing that right?"

"That's close enough. You can call me Tubby."

"Okay. But I'm not going to be seeing you anymore. I'm going home to Pennsylvania this afternoon. If you'll just wait over there with those other guys, you'll receive your protective attire and get your instructions for the day."

"What's the pay?"

"Fifteen dollars an hour."

Bonner smiled.

"And you'll earn it."

23

THE JOB WAS CLEANING OUT THE PUBLIC LIBRARY ON Harrison Avenue. All the guys wore the same white suits. There were some Koreans and Chinese, and an old black man without teeth, and two more Mexicans. Bonner was the only white guy.

All they had to do was carry wet books to the dumpster, and there were tons of wet books. It was easy work, except that it was difficult to breathe through the masks, so they all took them off. Except when they went outside. The boss said they couldn't be seen outside without their masks on.

Lunch was on the Salvation Army, from Rochester, New York, which set up a mobile kitchen outside in the street. They got ravioli and white bread, a candy bar, and as many packs of chips as they wanted. The Army also gave away two-pound sacks of peanuts. They had a box of stuffed animals, and some of the workers took those and stashed them with their little piles of free goodies outside on the brown lawn. For drinks there were ice chests full of water and Mountain Dews and other donated brands from around America that Bonner had never seen before.

He pulled out non-fiction all day. The numbers on the shelves were 400.1 to 700.5. It all went to the dumpster.

The company was called America's Clearest Environment. They even provided tents for everybody in City Park, but you had to pay five dollars to take a shower.

This last fact got Bonner into another altercation. He wasn't aware of the rule. When he decided to bathe after a couple of days on the job, he just blew off the demand for payment made by the attendant. The guy was a licensed electrician (he said) who actually made more money running the showers, keeping everybody's laundry straight, and being in charge of the toilet paper than he ever had wiring factories. He had even invested in a Port-O-Vac from Wal-Mart at $19.99, which he used to clean up the workers' tents. Guys tipped him ten or twenty dollars. His name was Anthony, but everybody called him "Wire Nut." He even sold cigarettes and cold Coca-Colas out of his tent.

When Bonner walked into the shower trailer and didn't settle up in advance, the attendant didn't worry. He would just collect on the way out, or set up a line of credit in his spiral notebook where he logged what everybody owed him. He sat on the dryer, keeping an eye on one of his customer's clothes tossing around while neatly folding another man's work shirts and underwear.

When Bonner turned off the shower and opened the curtain to towel off, Wire Nut made his presence known.

"I got that floor cleaned up just before you got here," he said proudly. "It was all muddy. Nobody wants to take a shower on a muddy floor."

Bonner didn't bother to reply. He pulled on a new pair of white pants he had brought with him to the trailer.

Wire Nut whistled a Beatles tune and kept folding clothes.

Bonner finished getting dressed. He collected his soiled outfit, his wet towel and his soap, and he proceeded to leave.

"Uh, pardner, showers cost five dollars," Wire Nut said.

"For what?" Rivette asked, brushing past.

"The shower costs five bucks. That's what it costs." Wire Nut put a gentle hand on Bonner's shoulder.

The criminal knocked it away. "I ain't payin' five dollars for a shower," he said flatly.

"You can do it on time and settle up when you get paid," Wire Nut suggested.

Bonner jabbed his fingers in Wire Nut's chest and pushed him away so firmly that the attendant tripped backwards over a bench and fell down into his plastic bags of dirty laundry.

"Stay away from me, dude," he warned and marched outside into the dark tree-covered night.

Wire Nut got to his feet sputtering. "Don't try coming back here!" he yelled out the door. "Bathe in the lake, see how you like it." He was referring to the bayou aesthetically arranged around the barricaded New Orleans Museum of Art. Lacking any maintenance since the storm, the stream was now topped with foamy green algae in which empty milk cartons floated.

Bonner didn't worry about the shower incident. He just went back to his tent and played chess with one of the Mexicans until he got tired and went to sleep.

But Wire Nut didn't forget about it. You couldn't run a business and let people get away with not paying. To be certain of his footing, he checked again with his employer at America's Clearest Environment to be sure that everyone agreed he could refuse service to workers who didn't pay.

"That place is yours to run," the boss told him. "As long as you keep it clean and the boys don't suds up each other's backs, five dollars is okay. Why, are the men complaining?"

"No, just this one guy," Wire Nut said grimly.

"It's your business. Don't bother me about it," the boss said.

Wire Nut had a friend named Doug. They had worked together in Texas, Oklahoma, and Florida. Doug was a real electrician and built like a camel. That's what people said, because he had a humpback, but he was very strong. Wire Nut persuaded Doug that they needed to waylay this upstart hillbilly and teach him respect.

They laid their plans, and the next night Wire Nut loaded up the washing machine and dryer and started them running at the same time.

"How ya doin', Roberto," he called to one of the clean-up workers using the shower.

"I'm pulling on it as hard as I can," Roberto replied.

"Oh, you're being rude," Wire Nut said, and slipped out the door.

Doug was waiting outside with some pieces of two-by-four left over from constructing the stairs to the shower trailer.

They trotted off into the darkness.

"He just went to the can," Doug reported.

That was convenient, since the portable toilets were set behind a tall hedge, keeping them out of sight of the campground. There were six of them, and an extra one, a few feet off, reserved for "senoritas." There was some problem between America's Clearest Environment and the company that was supposed to pump out the toilets, and the result was that they were full, and highly fragrant, and no one stayed near them any longer than absolutely necessary.

They had just rounded the bushes, where they were hidden in the shadows, when Bonner came out of one of the yellow boxes, distracted by zipping up his pants and getting his belt fastened while trying to get away as fast as he could.

"Hah!" Doug exclaimed and whacked Bonner with his wooden club. The blow might have done more damage if it had caught Rivette on his skull, but it hit his back instead and had no obvious effect on their quarry. He swung around to face them. Wire

Nut charged in, swinging his own two-by-four, and Doug went for the knees.

Rivette reacted swiftly, capturing Wire Nut's plank as it descended upon him and jerking it out of his assailant's hands. Wire Nut went spinning away and landed on the ground. Doug took a boot to the nuts and also staggered backwards. Bonner cracked his captured weapon on top of Doug's forehead, and the camel went down on his knees. Blood flowed out of his ear and down his whiskery chin. Bonner advanced upon him, and Doug crawled away to save his life. He managed to get his legs under him and ran away into the deeper recesses of the park.

Bonner turned on Wire Nut, who was scrambling backwards crawfish-like trying to get into the hedge. The two-by-four descended onto Wire Nut's ankle, which caused him to jerk up and hug the pain. Bonner gave him two quick pops to the head. Boom, boom. Out goes the light.

Bonner put an ear to Wire Nut's mouth, checking for respiration. He was dead. Rivette had not intended to kill him, but he was not particularly disturbed by that outcome. Powerful hurricanes couldn't bother about all the little things. But dead bodies meant police, and police meant flight, and Bonner hadn't figured out where to fly to yet.

He pulled the so-called electrician's body out of the evergreens. Slinging the little man over his shoulder, Rivette trotted off, keeping well away from the campers who were walking in the shadows around the perimeter, talking on cell phones or drinking malt liquor.

There was only one street to cross, deserted at night, and after that Rivette was back in the flood zone he liked—empty houses, lost cats, piles of garbage, no street lamps. The fashion of the day in New Orleans was to put refrigerators out on the curb, taped shut with duct tape. Many bore spray-painted slogans condemning FEMA, the President of the United States, or the owner of the Saints football team. Rivette dropped Wire Nut's body beside a likely looking double-wide ice box. Someone had written, "MMMM Tastes Like Chicken" in red marker on the outside.

Bonner tore off the silver tape and opened the floor. Piles of rotten food cascaded out. Mindless of the blast of decay, he tore away the wire racks, spilling old milk and fuzzy vegetables onto the street. This left a nice-sized space. Just about the right size for a body.

Bonner packed Wire Nut inside, kicking the deceased's shoe with his own until it disappeared. He closed the door. Leaning against the condemned appliance to keep it shut, he reused the duct tape to seal it back up again. The stick-um held. Maybe tomorrow, he thought, I ought to pass this way and put some more tape around the edges. It wouldn't do to have Wire Nut fall out.

He wiped his white-gloved hands on his white paper pants and walked calmly back to the camp. He would have himself a nice hot shower, on the house.

24

THERE WAS SOME CONCERN IN THE CAMP ABOUT THE missing Wire Nut. Bonner was in the can and heard men cursing about their clothes still being dirty. Doug didn't come out of his tent. Bonner suited up and went to work as usual, though. He didn't think anybody had seen anything. Doug was too scared to talk, and today was payday.

His crew made good progress at the library. They took all the metal book shelves apart and stacked them neatly in the brown grass outside the building. Most of the shelves were rusty from sitting in seven feet of water for a week or so, but someone thought they might be salvageable, so onto the lawn they went. The men kept all the doors to the building open for ventilation, and a big generator-driven fan was running, so all the fungal spores could blow outside. The walls inside the reading room were quite pretty, Bonner thought, intricate patterns of blue, orange, silver and green, little life forms spreading out to eat the city.

When four o'clock came, they gathered around the boss's pickup truck on Canal Boulevard, all in white suits like North Pole explorers, and got their checks.

"Dubonnet," the boss called.

"Here." Rivette accepted the envelope.

Of course all the banks were closed on a Friday evening. There was a check cashing service run out of the back of a van at City Park, but the money-changers' servants charged nine percent. Rivette knew where there was a branch bank open uptown, by the Daiquiri Shop, and since tomorrow was Saturday and he didn't have to work, he decided to go there in the morning and get everything coming to him.

Now that Bonner had money coming in, a plan for the future was forming. It involved buying a car and traveling over to Mississippi, where he had heard there was a lot more hurricane work a man could get lost in. He wanted to see more of the storm. He could always steal a car, but he would still need money for gas, meals, and a regular grub stake The plan also involved his friend, Christine, coming along with him. Exactly how he would find her, and what it would take to persuade her to go, hadn't been worked out quite yet, but so far he had accomplished everything he had set his mind on doing. Just like his daddy had told him he would.

He saw Doug that evening, when they were both collecting their styrofoam platters of beef tips and noodles from the Salvation Army trailer, but the electrician avoided his eyes and slunk away to eat in his tent.

"Smart man," Bonner thought, but he didn't think that Doug would just forget about the whole thing. He would eventually tell about the fight, leaving out the part about who started it, and point a finger at yours truly.

Bonner began toying with ways to eliminate the problem. He didn't want anybody standing between him and getting the money he needed to clear out of Louisiana. It was great being allowed to walk around all day with a mask on his face. Nobody was ever going to catch him around here. But mucking out the public library was not his ultimate goal in life. Understanding the hurricane was.

On Saturday morning Bonner was up early. He put on his camouflage pants and a black T-shirt, then covered these with the same soiled white chemical suit and hat he had worn the day before on the job. No sense unwrapping a brand new suit. Management was starting to dock the men twelve bucks for each new outfit they needed. Most of the guys just kept using the same old ones, no matter how funky with mold and fungus they got. Most of them even used their coveralls for pillows at night. You couldn't wash them at the laundry trailer because they would disintegrate. Of course, there was also no attendant in the laundry trailer now, so no one used the machine unless he had time to stand guard over his clothes for fear they might get dumped on the floor or stolen. And there was no one around to sell detergent. Rivette thought he could move into that job if he didn't have a loftier ambition.

He grabbed his Saturday morning coffee from the Salvation Army mobile kitchen. Today there was a fresh-faced young girl he hadn't seen before handing out the cups. She said she was from a church group in Kansas, and would just be here for a week. She asked if Bonner had been displaced by the storm.

He said, "Yes, ma'am. You want to take a tour of the city?"

"I've already seen a lot," she said.

"I could show you a lot more," he told her.

Paycheck in his pocket, Bonner set off for Carrollton Avenue, the route to the good part of the city that was above the flood. He was armed, as he always was when he ventured out into the wilderness. The gun he had taken from the Place Palais security guard was in his real pants covered by his white suit, and he carried a Buck knife taped to his ankle under his sock.

The walk took him past lots of restaurants he wished were

open, because he was hungry. There was Angelo Brocato's Italian Ice, and K-Jean's Seafood, and New York Pizza, and Venezia Pizzeria, and the Flying Burrito, and the Lemon Grass Vietnamese, and Manuel's Hot Tamales, and the Tastee Donuts, and the Five Happiness Chinese, and a Popeye's, a Rally's, a Wendy's, and Ye Olde College Inn for po-boys.

Every one of them was messed up, crusty brown flood lines midway across the doors, plywood in some of the windows. There really were no signs of life anywhere, except for some "gutting guys" like himself who were clearing out the Catholic Book Store. They said *"Buenos dias, mi amigo."*

Bonner ignored them and walked on. The face protector hung around his neck on its elastic band. The day was warming up, and he was hot inside his suit, but these white garments were his identity. No, they concealed his identity. In any case, white suits were where it's at.

Eventually he reached a string of businesses, set among the trees and residences which lined the street. His paycheck was drawn on the First Alluvial Bank, and he knew right where that was.

The bank was open, and there was a line of cars half-way around the block trying to access the drive-up windows. Bonner paused to check that he had his ID, then he walked into the branch and got in line.

It wasn't a bad wait, about ten minutes. The man in front of him tried to get into a conversation about the white suit Bonner was wearing, asking him if he were contaminated, ha ha, and should they keep their distance, ha ha.

Bonner shrugged, pretending not to speak English. Nothing unusual about that in New Orleans these days.

The little girl behind the counter gave him a strained smile and said good morning. She was already stressed, though only half an hour into the job, because her Friday night had been a late one, spent at the just re-opened Tipitina's listening to Sunpie, and because every one of her customers so far had presented a problem such as an out-of-state check, a third-party check, a complaint about a service charge wrongly assessed while the account-holder was evacuated to Timbuktu, or wherever. The teller was also living with her sister in a one bedroom apartment in Harahan because her own apartment in Mid-City got flooded, and . . . the list went on.

But she was glad to see that Bonner was trying to cash a pay-check drawn on her own bank, which was about as simple as a transaction could get.

"Do you have an account with us, sir?" she asked politely.

Bonner had to clear his throat to say no. There was a painting on the wall behind her. It showed palm trees and golden sand. It was the beach. There were whitecaps, a blue sky, big clouds, and it came to him. That's where the hurricane belonged. That's where it came from. The beach. That's where he wanted to go.

The teller interrupted this revelation. "Could I please see your identification?"

"Sure," he managed to say. He slid his library card and deputy sheriff's permit under the bar and through the little window.

"You are Mr. Dubonnet?" she asked, staring at the name for the first time.

"Yeah, that's me," Bonner said.

The girl looked at the check.

"I'll be just one minute, sir. I have to see how much is in this account."

She took the check and Bonner's ID to her supervisor who was trying to fix one of the printers at the drive-up window.

Bonner watched this nervously.

It happened that this particular teller knew who Tubby Dubonnet was.

"And the signatures don't even match," she whispered to her supervisor. "It could be a stolen check."

The supervisor looked at the endorsement and compared it to the specimen on file at the bank. She wiped her hands on one of the paper napkins stacked next to the box of Krispy Kreme donuts one of the girls had brought.

"I see," she said, and pinched the documents in her fingers and led the way back to the teller window.

"I'm sorry, Mr. Dubonnet," she said in an overly polite tone. Her glasses wiggled above her nose. "But do you have a driver's license or any other form of identification?"

The young teller stood close behind, waiting to see how this would turn out.

Bonner knew right then the jig was up. They were not going to give him his money. They probably were not even going to give him back his check. He needed to go to the beach.

"I think I got what you want somewhere," he said while he slowly adjusted his chemical escape mask over his mouth and nose. Now there was nothing visible about him except his eyes and ears, and not much of them.

"It's right here."

He whipped the revolver out of his pocket and pointed it straight between the supervisor's eyes.

"This is a bank robbery, lady," he wheezed through his mouth-piece. "Put all the money you got right here in my hand."

"Give him the drawer, honey," the supervisor said.

"Dat man's robbin' da bank," the customer behind Rivette informed everyone in line around him. The normal decorum of the lobby disintegrated. The customers bashed into one another scrambling for the exits, and the ladies in the side office ran out to see what was happening. The other tellers ducked behind their counters, and the ones serving the drive-though customers screamed for help into their speakers and ran for the back room.

The girl in front of Rivette was nervously counting out twenties into his hand.

"Just give it all to me!" he demanded, admiring the scene he had created.

She gave him stacks of bills with paper wrappers, presenting Bonner with the problem of how to carry his loot.

"Give me a bag!" he yelled.

The teller looked blank.

"We don't have any bags," the supervisor explained. "Or maybe there's something in the back room. Would you like to wait while I go look?"

Bonner realized this was getting out of hand. The lobby was now empty except for one woman whose high-heeled shoes stuck out from under the customer service desk. He could practically feel the police on the way.

"Get on the floor, you!" he commanded the teller and her boss. Frantically he crammed the packs of bills under his jump suit and into the pockets of his regular pants. Some missed and slid down his leg where they were trapped by his elastic anklets.

Bonner discharged his gun one at one of the wall cameras zooming in on him, and, clumsy with money, he burst out of the bank.

He ran down a side street into what in normal times was a busy residential neighborhood. Now it was uninhabited because of the flood, except for one roofing crew and some men gutting out one of the homes. A fire had taken out a couple of houses on the block, and only their brick porches and solitary chimneys remained, towering over collapsed piles of burned timbers and rubble.

That is where Bonner hid himself, in one of the burned-out

shells. He immediately stripped off his white suit and tossed it aside. The money came pouring out. No sooner did it hit the ground than one of the packages of money exploded and showered his legs and much of the cash with blue dye. Now he looked like a house painter which was not such a bad disguise, but a lot of the bills looked like the fifty dollar play-money in a Monopoly game.

He kicked all of the cash, good and bad, under some roofing shingles and hid his white suit in the crawl space underneath what had been the porch. He heard sirens in the distance.

Rivette climbed out of the burned-out house and ambled down the block to where some men wearing little white dust masks were hauling wet sheetrock out of a home.

"Y'all need any help?" he asked.

The men spoke no English, but they pointed upstairs where he found the contractor sitting in the living room talking on his cell phone. He waited patiently until the man's call was finished, then asked him for a job.

"It's dirty work," the contractor said.

"I don't mind," Bonner told him, and nobody looking at him would doubt that. He had on a sweaty T-shirt, green and brown duck-hunters' pants, and blue paint stains from his knees to his toes. There were also white booties around his shoes, which gave him that professional "gutting" look.

"What's the job pay?" he asked.

"Ten bucks an hour."

"Can I start now?"

"Sure. Go on downstairs and pitch in."

Which is what he did, moving in step behind the other men who were tearing chunks of wet sheetrock off a wall and dumping it into wheelbarrows. He quickly got in the rhythm. The boss poked his head in the door and said he would be back in one hour. Bonner and one of the Latinos each took charge of a full wheelbarrow and rolled them out to the street where they were building a great pile of refuse.

A patrol car approached. A police lady wearing aviator sunglasses leaned out the window.

"You see anybody in a white suit come running by here," she asked.

The Latino worker almost bolted. Seeing no escape, however, he controlled himself and smiled *"No hablo Ingles,"* he said and pointed at Bonner.

"I didn't see anything," Bonner said.

"If you see anyone strange, call us. There was a bank robbery in the next block."

"Will do," Bonner replied. The police car drove slowly away.

The Latino smiled at him and shrugged.

Bonner shrugged back. No, there weren't any strange people around here.

25

TUBBY GOT A PERSONAL VISIT FROM DETECTIVE JOHNNY Vodka. The lawyer was on his stomach, replacing another wall outlet he thought might have gotten wet in the hurricane.

"The door's unlocked," he called out when he heard the knock.

Vodka obliged. "Are you all right down there?" he asked, standing over Tubby.

"Oh, it's you. Yeah, I'm just doing some wiring." He got to his feet and dusted his trousers off.

"Have you been robbing banks, Mr. Dubonnet?" the policeman asked.

"No, I'm too dumb for that, except that I have represented banks and charged as much as I could get away with. Why the question?"

"At 9:58 this morning a man presented a check made out to you at the First Alluvial Bank on Carrollton, and when they wouldn't cash it he stuck up the place."

"It wasn't me."

"I knew it wasn't you. The teller says she knows you, and that's why she wouldn't cash the check. Besides, the robber was described as tall and thin. That lets you off the hook."

Tubby knew it was true. He considered himself reasonably tall, but since he started wrestling in the 180-pound class in high school, nobody had ever called him thin.

The policeman filled Tubby in on what had happened.

"Why was he using my name?"

"Don't you see? He's bound to be your boy. I got a description from the people he worked for, some clean-up crew over in City Park, and he sounds just like Bonner Rivette. We took some prints from the bank, and I'll bet you a bag of beignets they come back a match."

"So he is still around," Tubby said. He wiped his brow,

"Sure is, and close by, too. He's still on the loose, and get this. They found the security man at your office building, the Place Palais, across the street in the Bunny Biscuit with a concussion. He's in a coma. The man's name is Manuel . . ."

"Manuel Oteza. I've known him for years. He let me into my office the day before the storm hit."

"Right. Of course, it could be a coincidence, but I make Bonner Rivette a suspect. He hasn't tried to contact you?"

"Hell, no!" It was now apparent to Tubby that this Rivette individual was a banshee that had been released by the storm.

"Or your daughter? What's her name?"

"Christine. No. There's been no contact."

"Do you think he might know where you live?"

"Of course he could. He's been in my office. Christ, I'm in the phone book."

"Then you might want to lock your doors and not just let people like me come walking in."

That was helpful. "Sure, I see what you're saying." Tubby's mind was seething. Maybe his somber imagination was right. Maybe there was evil afoot, and just maybe it had the Dubonnet family's number.

Not an hour after Vodka had left, the call came in. It was from Christine, and she was hysterical.

"He phoned me, Daddy. That same man."

"Rivette?" Tubby knew whom she meant.

"Yes," she shrieked. "I answered the phone, and there he was. He asked me if I had a place where he could stay."

"If you had a place?" Tubby knew he sounded dumb.

"Yes. He said he didn't have a place to stay. And then he said we could take a trip together."

"Where are you now?"

"I'm driving back to town with my friend, Samantha. We're on the Interstate coming home."

"To this house?"

"Actually, I was planning to stay with Samantha in an apartment she's got on First Street. The landlord told her the electricity was turned on and she had to start paying rent."

Christine was calming down. "She asked if I would move in and share."

Tubby's mind raced nowhere. Was Christine safer back in Jackson, Mississippi? Would she be safer with him where he could keep watch? Had Samantha started talking again?

"Has Samantha begun to talk yet?"

"She's starting to, Daddy. I think she'll be normal soon."

"Who knows her address?"

"Huh? Well, I guess she does. I'll ask her."

"No! No!" Tubby shouted. "I'm not being clear. What I mean is, Rivette's been involved in a bank robbery and possibly killing people. He's very dangerous. If you stay at Samantha's, is there any way he would know where you are?"

"I don't see how. I didn't know where I was going until today."

"Look, you call me every hour until you get here. There's a

policeman interested in this case. I'll ask him what he thinks you should do."

"Okay. He sounded real creepy. It was just the strange way he acted like there was nothing wrong. Like it was the most natural thing to call me out of the blue. Like he was asking me out for a date."

"What did you say to him?"

"I told him no, he couldn't stay with me. I asked him if he thought I was nuts."

"And?"

"He laughed and said he'd bet I would like the beach."

"The beach?!" Now Tubby was shouting.

"Really. Who goes to the beach in October?"

Tubby counted to three silently. "If he calls back, don't speak to him, okay?"

"It might be one way to find him, Daddy, if I do talk with him some."

"Yeah, well don't."

"I'm scared of him. I think about his 'I am Katrina' thing all the time."

"Well, he's not Katrina," Tubby said. Or maybe he was—just as senseless, just as out of control. "I'm going to hang up and call the police."

"Okay. Love you."

Tubby told her he loved her, too.

He called the number Johnny Vodka had given him. It rang, but no answer. He called the number of the First District Police. Detective Vodka was not in. They would give him a message.

He opened the front door and looked outside. It was nighttime now. He had the yard almost cleared of branches. Only one twenty-foot length of magnolia trunk still lay across the lawn. It was more than a foot in diameter, and he had not had a chance to whack it up into manageable pieces with his chain saw. There were lots of places to hide in his yard, lots of places he couldn't see. None of the streetlights on the block were working yet. His daughters meant so much to him. Even though he might not be such a prize, his daughters made up for it. They had to be shielded from harm. Christine had already had a narrow escape from Rivette's clutches. He didn't believe she had even told him the whole story of what the man had done to her. She was such a sweet smart girl. Nothing more could happen to her.

He had always derived great strength from his place in New Orleans, his network of friends, his seat at the bar. Now it was broken, dispersed, in disarray. He had never felt so powerless, so all alone, so angry.

BONNER RIVETTE put in a good day's work, and the boss handed him three twenty-dollar bills out in front of the house they were gutting, two blocks away from the First Alluvial Bank he had robbed.

"Tomorrow morning, eight o'clock, right here," he told his crew, and everybody said yes, sir. With the downstairs stripped almost to the walls and the upstairs green with creeping mold, the contractor did not bother to lock the place. There was nothing inside anybody would want to steal.

"I'm waiting for my ride," Bonner informed everybody and sat on the steps. After the rest of the men left, he remained there for another half an hour picking dirt off his clothes. When it started to get dark he ambled down the sidewalk to the burned-out shell of a building where he had hidden his money. He climbed back into the charred ruin and kicked aside the roofing shingles that covered his hoard.

A lot of the money was stained with the blue dye and he didn't feel safe carrying it around. But there also were many uncontaminated bills, and he collected those into his pockets. The white chemical suit was his ally, so he retrieved that as well.

Attempting to be as inconspicuous as possible, he went back to the house where he had been working all day. He went upstairs to investigate.

There was some furniture—a sofa, mattresses on the bedroom floor, the ubiquitous kitchen refrigerator. The homeowner had apparently already removed everything he desired, like tables and bed frames, consigning the rest to curbside pick-up by the disaster contractors. Among the abandoned tins of spices and bottles of Log Cabin syrup in the pantry, he found a few edibles. There was an unopened jar of Tabasco pepper jelly, a can of Campbell's Split Pea with Ham and Bacon soup, and even a vacuum-sealed canister of cashew pieces and bits from Walgreens. Whatever he didn't take was going onto the street tomorrow. This place fit him, and he bedded down for the night.

He thought about lighting a candle, but decided that he preferred the darkness and the solitude of an empty house in an empty neighborhood. Two blocks away there was light, and the glow reminded him of the human race at the gates. If they invaded his space, he would invade theirs. Given just a little time, he would be moving on anyway, further east on the Gulf Coast where the waterfront was blown clear of inhabitants, where the houses had been reduced to piles of splintered lumber and stone and the woods were full of furniture. To the beach. Where the storm was still strong. Christine would be with him there. As long as she could stay away from that preacher. No, that was his sister. He had momentarily mixed them up. Christine would be there with him, and together they would keep the energy of the wind alive.

He slept on the floor, and he was meditating outside the front door the next morning when the boss showed up.

"Man, I like this," the boss said. "It's good to have someone you can count on."

Since it was Sunday, they only put in half a day. In the course of clearing out a bedroom, Bonner had found a cardboard box of clothes. A pair of pants fit him well enough that he was able to discard his blue leggings into the trash heap. He still had a clean white suit in a bag, but he would save that.

When they broke off at lunch, Bonner packed his gear. The boss told him to be sure to show up tomorrow morning, and he said he would, though he had an entirely different plan.

He knew where Christine's father lived. The address was on the library card, and it was an easy walk away.

His route took him past a neighborhood restaurant that had just re-opened. Only one of the tables outside was occupied, and the man there was drinking coffee behind his *New York Times*. Bonner felt safe enough to go inside and order a ham and cheese sandwich to go. The Middle Eastern proprietor tried to start a conversation about the Saints game he was watching on television—a Saints game from their new home in San Antonio—but Bonner played dumb. He paid for his sandwich and took it with him to eat while he walked.

He passed a house where some college-student types were sunning in lawn chairs in the yard, using storm debris, decorated with Mardi Gras beads, as a table for their beer. Bags of trash and two old refrigerators were on the curb in front. There was a Suzuki motorcycle sitting in the driveway with a "For Sale" sign taped to its handlebars.

Bonner kept going for half a block while the scene percolated around in his head, and then he reversed course.

"Who's selling the bike?" he asked.

One of the boys raised his sunglasses. "That would be me," he said.

"How much do you want?" Bonner asked.

"It's in good shape. Didn't even get wet in the flood. I'm asking $3,900."

"I can see the mud on the spokes, dude. Does it run?"

"Oh, yeah. I wouldn't sell it but I need the cash 'cause I lost my job at Commander's. They're closed, so what can I do? No, this bike is a honey."

"Let's hear it crank up."

The guy was barefoot and in a bathing suit, but he managed to fire his Suzuki up. It made a great blast, with only a couple of erratic coughs.

"Might be some bad gas," he said.

"Let me try it out," Bonner said.

"Sure." The boy tried to relieve Bonner of his pillow-case pouch, but his customer jerked it back and glared.

"We be cool, dude," the athlete said. "Just bring back my bike."

Bonner took it for a spin around the block. The motorcycle ran okay as long as it was above 4,000 RPMs. It had a hard time idling. And he did bring it back.

"I'll give you $2,000."

"Oh, man . . ."

They settled at $2,700.

Bonner went into his pack and pulled out the money.

The kid was surprised but not averse to be receiving cash money. He even had a title to the motorcycle. "How shall I fill it out?" he asked.

"Just sign it," Bonner said.

"I guess we're supposed to have a notary do this."

"Don't sweat the small stuff. I ain't worried about it."

And he did a wheelie roaring off down the street.

TUBBY DID NOT THINK there was anything amiss when he went to visit Christine's new apartment in the Garden District. It was about a ten-minute drive away in one of the city's nicest sections. To say that the area had been spared by the storm would be incorrect. Elephant-sized trees lay dead on the sidewalk, waiting for the heavy-duty equipment to arrive and truck them away. Roofing slate was piled high on the curb, and refrigerators were everywhere, but there had been no flood here. Most of the houses showed signs of life.

The building where Christine lived was a duplex, finished in mauve stucco. Its two entrances were announced by boxwood hedges and framed charmingly by once-functional gas lights. He rang the bell, and was momentarily surprised that the chimes worked. He had become unused to normal electrification. Samantha answered the door in pajamas and a robe. She apologized for not being dressed at two o'clock in the afternoon, but said that they were cleaning house today. Christine was upstairs vacuuming. Come on in.

Tubby went, inhaling with satisfaction the air of an old house scented with young ladies' soaps. He was so used to the mustiness and rot of his own part of the city that he felt as though he were on a vacation to some wonderful resort far away on the globe.

"We have some coffee, and there may be some croissants left over, Mr. Dubonnet," Samantha said, leading him up to their clean and orderly kitchen. She spoke quite distinctly as if each word were important to her.

Not once had Tubby noticed the motorcyclist trailing him on Prytania Street. The fact that the bike had stopped when he did and pulled into a parking spot down the block had completely escaped him.

26

JOHNNY VODKA CALLED TUBBY THE NEXT MORNING TO report that a twenty-dollar bill heisted by Bonner Rivette from the First Alluvial Bank had turned up in the deposit envelope dropped off at the bank by the Najaf Deli on Freret Street. It didn't lead to much, Vodka said. He had already been over to the Najaf, and the owner said he remembered nothing about the customer.

"You know, the typical thing. He doesn't know a squid from a sea bass. He probably doesn't even have a Health Department permit to open the restaurant. Or he might, I don't know. I threatened him a little bit, but it didn't improve his recollections any. He might have seen Rivette, or he doesn't know. The point is, we know that Rivette is around, and very close by."

"My daughter's in town. She's hidden away," Tubby said. "If he comes around here, I'm carrying a gun."

"That's fine. It's every man for himself these days. If you see this character, you can call me or shoot him yourself, whatever you can do."

"Can't we get more manpower, maybe the FBI or something?" Although threatening to pack heat, Tubby was not truly ready to assume all of the responsibilities of law enforcement.

The line was silent.

"Okay, I was just asking," Tubby said.

"You got to understand, Mr. Dubonnet. This is a national disaster. We ain't exactly got what you call a lot of resources. I wouldn't even have known about the money turning up if the bank manager wasn't related to my captain. I'm just saying this so you'll understand."

"Yeah. Well, I appreciate whatever you can do."

"Sure. I'll let you know when I find out something, and you do the same. If you do happen to shoot him, call me right away."

"I got that part," Tubby said.

Sardis Sanitary Supply, sub-sub-contractor in charge of appliance removal in zip code 70119, was working Florida Street. Its three inspectors worked seven days a week. Their company got two hundred dollars per refrigerator located, then more money to cart it off for refrigerant removal, then more for electrical wiring removal, then more to drop it at the refrigerator dump. At that point another company would take over and get paid to crush the white-goods into cubes for recycling. The street inspectors earned two hundred dollars a day, and were delighted to have it, even if they had to live in an old Winnebago parked at an Interstate rest area thirty miles north of town.

Jack Shimlechek had been a community college professor of biology in Crampon, Indiana, when he learned about this job on the web, his late-night companion. He did the math and was en route to the sunny south twenty-four hours later. The college simply cancelled his course.

During his career teaching at the high school level and in college, he had watched the dissection of thousands of chickens, frogs and mice, but he had never encountered anything so earthy and nostril-filling as the endless population of curb-side refrigerators in New Orleans. The worse it got, and the more his partners gagged, the more he laughed. He was a good leader for his men, two former elementary-school counselors from Nashville.

His humor was tested when he used a utility knife to take off the duct tape on a nice double-wide icebox. He stepped a few paces back and retired to his knees for personal reasons.

His assistant who carried the paper work came to help, took a look in the box and also went to sit down on the curb.

"Old Rocky Top," he whistled, nonsensically. "Rocky Top, Tennessee."

"JUST LETTING YOU KNOW," Vodka told Tubby on the telephone, "I think we got your boy linked up an actual murder."

Tubby's nerves were numb. His face was granite. "Who is it this time?"

"Some laborer who stayed up at the campground in City Park. A guy they called Wire Nut. He was stuffed inside a refrigerator."

"That's unusual." He was sweating. His concentration was failing.

"You know, you're right. We haven't had too many refrigerator murders that I can think of offhand. It may be unique. Or maybe this is just the start of a trend."

"Does this bring you any closer to catching him?"

"Not really. I haven't got a clue where the guy is hiding himself. I'm just letting you know he's leaving lots of crapola behind him wherever he goes."

"Yes, indeed."

"I mean, we're looking for him," Vodka said defensively. "It's just, he ain't the only thing out there, and we're still not up to strength at the police department."

"I get it," Tubby said. He was tired of hearing about all the problems. Law and order were out the window. I mean, let's just find this guy and pop him. Simple as that.

STEVE AND GASTRO didn't have much to do on Monday morning so they decided to drive up to New Orleans to see if Gastro could find any of his old friends.

"Funny how this all looks so normal," Steve commented as he piloted his Frontier up the entrance ramp to the Westbank Expressway.

"The Home Depot's sign blew down," Gastro pointed out.

"Sure, they had lotsa wind, but everybody's back in business."

They got in line to pay their toll at the Crescent City Connection Bridge and had time to check out most of the radio stations on the dial before they finally got to the toll plaza, it was that crowded.

"Look how many cars is from Texas. Guess I should come back up here and get another job," Steve said unenthusiastically. "I liked working for Mr. Flowers. Maybe he's got something else for me."

"If I can find a certain somebody, I might be able to get some weed to sell," Gastro suggested helpfully.

"I don't know about that," Steve said, "But you tell me where you want to go."

They took the first exit off the bridge and did stop-and-go into the French Quarter. The traffic lights still weren't operating, and some drivers had trouble understanding that they didn't have to sit all day waiting for a four-way stop sign to change. Finally they crossed Canal and grabbed a place to park on Chartres Street. The sign said "Loading Zone," but it was hard to believe that anybody was issuing tickets.

"My old hang-out's Jackson Square," Gastro said, and he led

them walking in that direction. The October afternoon was warm. Steve had a cut-off wife-beater T-shirt over his blue jeans. Gastro had on black pants and a black button-up shirt, and looked like the caricature of a geek, though his face had so many wires implanted in it he should have been able to receive e-mails.

They strolled into the Square, where the stately Cabildo and Presbytere were still blocked off behind a plywood wall and most of the shops, even La Madeleine's coffee and *croque monsieur*, were locked up.

"This is dismal," Gastro said.

He brightened when he saw one tarot card reader plying her trade. Normally there were at least ten. And though he didn't customarily relate to the portrait painters who had once hung their work on every available spot of iron fence, he was kind of glad to see that at least one had returned and even had a customer, a man who looked like George Bush, and who was having himself rendered in charcoal, en profile.

Two young men were playing guitars together on a bench, and Gastro tapped Steve on the shoulder to make him stop and listen. The musicians were also dressed in black and wore their hair long. There was an upturned cowboy hat on the cobblestones where contributions might be made.

They were having a hard time finding a tune they both knew, but approached the task seriously.

"You guys know where 'Blues Rap' is?" Gastro interrupted.

They looked him over.

"Don't know who you're talking about, dude," one of them said in a strong western accent.

Gastro walked off, and Steve had to hurry to catch up.

"Those guys are not even from here," Gastro complained.

"Well, man, you ain't from here either," Steve reminded him.

"I paid my dues in New Orleans," Gastro said haughtily. "Those kids probably came in here after the hurricane."

Steve followed his friend through the French Market, where there were only a few stands selling sunglasses, and over to Royal Street, which was deserted. Gastro's eyes darted left and right at every intersection.

Finally he sat down on the curb.

"This sucks," the street ranger said.

"What's the matter, man?"

"Nobody's around. It's all empty."

"We ain't even knocked on no doors, dude. How you gonna find your friend if you don't go to his house?"

Gastro looked at him like he was from another planet.

"Most of my friends don't have no stupid houses or apartments. They hang on the streets, like we're doing now. Only we're the only ones hanging here."

That was certainly true.

"The whole counterculture is gone. It's someplace else. It isn't here," Gastro griped. "This is just empty city. This could be . . . like . . . Montgomery on a Sunday afternoon!" He couldn't come up with anything worse.

"I hadn't ever been to Montgomery."

"I wonder where everybody went," Gastro said, leaning back against a fluted cast iron column, feeling discouraged.

"You mean to tell me you lived here how long? A year at least. And you have friends, and you don't know where a single one of them lives?" Steve was having trouble comprehending this.

Gastro was too bummed to answer.

"At least let's go have some fun," the big fellow said. "I can find Bourbon Street, that's for sure."

He got up and started walking, and Gastro scooped himself out of his miasma and followed behind.

"Look," Steve said as they got closer to the scene and encountered more people, "why don't we call Mr. Dubonnet's daughter, Christine, and see if she wants to come down and party with us? Maybe she's got a girlfriend."

"I don't care either way," Gastro said. Yet the appearance of open bars and people stuffing pizza in their mouths as they walked was restorative.

"Okay then. I got her number in my phone."

Steve leaned against a wire trash can and tapped the keypad of his pocket wonder.

"Yeah, hello, this is Steve Oubre. You remember me? From Petrofoods and all that? Sure. Listen, are you doing anything this evening? Me and Gastro . . ."

Christine arranged to meet them at a club Gastro suggested called the Dirty Dungeon to hear a band called the Breaded Sisters at eight o'clock. Since there was a curfew at 2:00 AM, the bands had to start playing early. She would try to bring her roommate Samantha.

Meanwhile Steve and Gastro had a couple of hours to kill. They pooled their money, which came to sixty-eight dollars, and decided that gave them enough to drink a few beers, so they walked around taking in the sights. It was after five o'clock and at least Bourbon Street was alive with foot traffic. There was a crowd outside the Famous Door. Music poured from the clubs as the day's sun went down. Everyone was sporting a plastic cup of beer, and the voices were loud.

"This is the strangest thing," Steve said, swallowing his Dixie draft. He didn't realize it had been kegged before the hurricane flooded the brewery.

"I've never seen this before," Gastro said.

Everybody on the street was male.

They promenaded on Bourbon Street in both directions. They

mixed and mingled and stopped to peer into the music joints and to soak up the Dixieland Jazz and the smells of shrimp frying, but there wasn't a woman in sight.

"These boys are all from Texas," Steve said.

"They're all Mexicans, you ask me," was Gastro's view.

"Whoo. There's a lot of them. They ain't no fair sex at all. We're gonna have to protect our ladies tonight. These muchachos must be mighty lonely."

27

THE DIRTY DUNGEON ON ESPLANADE AVENUE WAS VERY crowded at seven-thirty when Gastro and Steve swaggered in. The juke box was playing loudly. The Breaded Sisters had not yet started their gig. Gastro finally found someone he knew, a bearded chemist with some sort of terminal disease that he rarely mentioned, and which had obviously not yet killed him. They screamed at each other over the noise. Steve watched the door, waiting for Christine and her friend to arrive.

At half past eight Christine showed up alone. This caused a minor sensation at the bar because she was almost the only female in the place. Steve had been on the alert, and he pushed his way through the crowd to claim the woman.

"It's great to see you." He gave her a bear hug. "Your friend didn't come?"

"She'll probably come later. She wants me to call her and tell her what kind of scene this is."

"It's Gastro's scene, whatever you call it. If it was me we'd go out for country music. See, he already found somebody he knows."

Steve directed Christine to a little table against the wall that Gastro and the chemist, wearing a red baseball cap backwards, were using for an ashtray. The guy with the cap melted away as they arrived. Gastro said "Hi" to Christine and confided to Steve that, "The dude might be able to help us."

The juke box was playing Nine Inch Nails.

"This is the first time I've been out since I got back to New Orleans." Christine had to shout to make herself heard.

"You wanna beer?" Steve asked.

She said fine, anything would do. Mindful that his treasury was getting thin, Steve barged his way to the bar in search of whatever was cheapest.

"Well, tell me what you've been doing since the last time I saw you," Christine said to Gastro.

He blushed from the attention, but no one saw that in the dim Dungeon.

"Not much," he said. "How about you?"

"Okay, well first I went to stay with my father at his house for a few days, and that was fine. We just worked to clean things up, but you know that, and then I went . . . ."

BONNER RIVETTE WEDGED his motorcycle between two parked cars on Esplanade Avenue. He had tracked Christine as she drove from her apartment to the French Quarter and had seen her go into the bar. This was the right time to make contact, he decided, since she was on foot and it was suitably dark.

The question was whether to follow her into the bar, and he pondered that for half an hour. Rivette was reclined against his chrome seat back, but he was quite aware of what was going on around him. He recognized the television show blaring from a nearby house, "The Simpsons." He heard a man walking his dog down the sidewalk a block away. Rivette was wearing his new white chemical suit and white gloves for his night on the town. The paper bonnet and his respirator mask were in his pouch, and he could always put those on if he went into the club.

As it turned out, Christine came to him.

THE SMOKE AND CLOSENESS of the bar were getting to Christine.

"I'm going outside to call my friend Samantha," she told her two escorts and pushed off, fiddling in her bag for her cell phone. Outside the air was sweet, and she shook her hair to get some of the cigarette smell out.

She flipped open the phone and found speed dial to connect to her roommate.

"Hello, Christine. What's it like?"

"It's not too bad. There's lots of boys. Why don't you come down?"

"I don't know if I'm really up for loud music."

"Come on. You haven't been out for months. If you don't like it we can go somewhere else."

"I don't know. I'm watching an old re-run of the 'Brady Bunch.'"

"I'M GOING OUTSIDE to check on Christine," Gastro said. "This isn't the best neighborhood in the world." Even as he said this he realized that he was caring about Christine, and that caring about someone was not how you normally survived.

"Tell her the band's about to start," Steve called to his back.

CHRISTINE FELT THE TAP on her shoulder and turned around to see Bonner Rivette. She shrieked.

"What's happening?" her roommate on the phone asked.

"It's him! Call my daddy! Call my daddy!" was all Christine could say before the criminal knocked the phone out of her hand.

She tried to bolt, but he fastened his grip onto both of her arms.

"Don't scream, Christine," he said soothingly. "I just want to talk to you."

"You go to hell!" She struggled, but he pulled her further from the bar and its lights.

He was very strong, just as she'd remembered, and he succeeded in muffling her voice against his chest as he dragged her past the quiet houses and under the live oak trees. She tried to kick at him with her sneakers and knee him in the groin, but he clutched her so tightly that she couldn't make it work. It was like they were two lovers dancing in slow motion down the sidewalk.

TUBBY WAS DRIVING his big Chrysler near Lee Circle when he got the call. He had been on a mission to make copies of his insurance claim forms at Kinko's, but he had failed, not realizing that the once twenty-four-hour-a-day establishment was now open only from nine to three on weekdays because of a labor shortage.

"Mr. Dubonnet!" It was the excited voice of Christine's room-mate, finally talking. "That awful man has got her again."

She told him what she knew and where Christine was.

He tore at the wheel, knuckles white, blaring his horn through stop signs, racing for the French Quarter. He tried to press 911 while he steered, but his fingers couldn't find the numbers.

GASTRO DID NOT SEE CHRISTINE when he stepped out of the bar. He thought she might have ditched the party and taken herself home. He was disappointed, but then people often treated him that way. Since he had come outside to see to her safety, however, he waited for a minute to see if anything appeared to be amiss. His eye caught a movement down the street, and he moseyed that way. And then he heard the muffled scream and began to run.

Bonner Rivette had Christine in the driveway of a tall deserted house. Pieces of its roof lay about the pavement. His motorcycle was right across the street, and he was trying to squeeze enough air out of the girl so that she would listen to what he had to say.

Like it or not, she was going to ride with him to the Gulf Coast. They were going to blow this city, even if he had to kill her to get her there.

He saw Gastro but perceived him to be a minor problem. Still holding Christine tightly by the arm with his left hand, Rivette prepared his right to take care of the hippy squirt.

Gastro yelled, "What's going on?" but he didn't wait for an explanation. He flailed his way in like a windmill, the only tactic that had ever worked for him in high school. Bonner sought to use Christine as a shield, but that started her swinging and kicking at him, too, so he threw her roughly onto the driveway. Then he could use both hands on the kid. One, two, three, and Gastro was on the ground with a broken nose.

"Helpless little woman, am I?" Christine screamed. "Your soul mate, am I?" She had a brick from a fallen chimney in her hand, and she clocked Rivette on the side of the head with it. He sank to one knee, and looked at her curiously.

"I'm just someone to knock around, right?" she shouted and whacked him again. Bonner rolled away trying to control the pain. Blood from his forehead was coloring his white suit.

Christine threw her brick at him and picked up another one. Gastro was back up on his knees, shaking his head to clear it. A car screeched to the curb, horn blasting, and Rivette staggered to his feet. It was time to flee.

He ran behind Tubby's Chrysler as the lawyer was leaping out. Christine pegged another brick which missed Bonner by several feet but which indicated to her father that she was bravely alive. He turned to give chase, but Bonner already had his Suzuki running. He kicked it onto gear and aimed himself down Esplanade Avenue.

"You're not getting away again," Tubby shouted and jumped back behind the wheel of his car. He burned rubber in pursuit while Christine, breathing heavily, tenderly used Gastro's shirt to mop his crooked nose.

BONNER WASN'T FEELING SO GOOD. He could make his Suzuki go fast, but he could not steer it so well. He thought his skull might be fractured, it hurt that bad. He blinked and almost ran over the curb into the shuttered Café du Monde. He righted his course. Headlights stabbed at his eyes. Drivers swerved to miss him.

More pain rushed through his right shoulder, almost causing him to crash high-speed into the iron fence around Jackson Square. Why, he'd been shot! That bastard father of Christine's was shooting at him!

Indeed Tubby was firing away, big slugs from his .45—twenty-five years of practicing law forgotten. Nor was he the least concerned about winging bystanders, so it was lucky that the few about were Texans who knew how to take cover from a gunfight. Anytime he got within a hundred feet of the motorcycle's taillights he pulled the trigger and the gun kicked hard. Since he was aiming out the window with his left hand, it was pure luck that he got anything into Rivette at all. Tubby had never fired a weapon at a human being before, but he had lost his mind over this one. He was cursing nonstop through his beard, intent on keeping the Suzuki in view. All he wanted was a chance to ram the son of a bitch and run him over.

Rivette went left between a parking lot and the Jax Brewery, lured there by the absence of street lights. His mind was blanking out. Tubby saw the turn and came around the corner on two tires. The street crossed the railroad tracks and ended in a small parking lot beside the Moon Walk, the little park for lovers and street musicians built atop the levee. It rambled above the rocky artificial shore of the Mississippi River. The railroad's wooden crossing arm was down, but Rivette maneuvered his motorcycle around it. Tubby slammed on the brakes and slid to a halt next to the tracks.

He was out of the car, running after Rivette with his pistol still clutched in his hand. The criminal was just ahead. His bike, idling noisily, was pointed up the slope of the levee. Tubby hoped Rivette wasn't dead yet because he wanted to shoot him himself.

Bonner's strength was waning. The fire was going out. The wind inside was dying down. All he wanted to do was fly, high as he once had, clearing everything from his path. He heard that lawyer, Dubonnet, panting and cursing behind him. He gave the throttle a mighty twist and stomped the bike into gear.

He got the traction and came over the top of the levee with his speedometer sweeping toward sixty miles per hour. It went to the end of the gauge when the back tire came off the grass and Rivette sailed into the sky.

Running right behind him, Tubby clicked his useless empty gun repeatedly as Bonner soared over the rocks. He saw Rivette arc over the current and hit the water with a splash that seemed so silent because the engine roar extinguished, echoing away. The lawyer watched the motorcycle bubble around for one tiny moment before it sank beneath the surface. Bonner's body detached. It floated away, a lump of blackness that quickly disappeared in the dark of the river.

"I didn't know the gun was loaded," Tubby sang to himself. "And I'll never do it again."

THERE WERE NO RECRIMINATIONS from the police department. Johnny Vodka said he would notify Tubby as soon as Bonner Rivette's body washed up. "It can't be long," he assured him. "That river's got so many poisons in it he'll die if he only had a little bitty scratch."

28

THE SKY BEGAN TO BRIGHTEN. TUBBY HELD THAT THOUGHT, watching the sun come up over the stubble of his trees. Christine and Gastro, after he had got his nose splinted at Touro Hospital, came to stay with him for a few days to recuperate. Camp Dubonnet now had electricity, water, and gas, and was starting to seem like a real home again.

"This is a really nice place you got, Mr. Dubonnet," Gastro told him while they were cleaning the breakfast dishes together. Tubby had fixed a big cheese omelet for everybody, and now Christine was upstairs showering and getting dressed.

Using a brick on Bonner Rivette might have restored something in her. She did not avoid your eyes anymore when she spoke to you. She talked confidently about the forthcoming semester at Tulane. She had found some old jogging shoes from high school and taken them out for a run.

"Yeah, I guess things are getting better, Gastro. A little bit better each day."

"That's what Steve's folks say down in the country. Except they don't have jobs."

"I don't actually have a job, either. That's still a problem."

"Don't you have clients? I mean, you're a lawyer, right?" Gastro couldn't believe that a lawyer would ever encounter any real hardships in life.

"I had clients, buddy, but I don't know where most of them are. A lot of their houses got flooded, and I'm sure they're spread out all over the country. Some of them have probably found something better than they had here. They'd be smart not to come back." And truth was, Tubby wasn't really sure that he still wanted to be a lawyer.

"You mean that? Why wouldn't they come back? New Orleans is a great place to live. It's pretty. It's very interesting."

"I didn't know you had those kinds of ideas Sid, I mean Gastro. You think it's pretty? Hey, you lived in the gutter, right?"

"Close," Gastro said. "But I've been noticing the scenery lately. And the people around here aren't so bad."

"Maybe it's that post-hurricane friendliness," but Tubby knew that wasn't true. People in New Orleans had always called you "honey" and "darling" even if you were just buying a loaf of bread.

Since the phones were working pretty well now, he called Hope.

She answered, and he liked hearing her voice.

"Uh," he paused, then charged ahead. "I thought you might want to come over for dinner tonight," he said.

"Well, maybe."

"I've got Gastro and Steve Oubre here, and Christine's here, and if you came it would be kind of like a reunion."

"All the refugees in town at once."

"Not all. That would be way too many to feed. But I've got a sack of oysters."

"Yuck. From the Gulf? After the hurricane? No way?"

He was a little bit disappointed, but he had anticipated this eventuality.

"I've also got a couple of pounds of smoked sausage I'm gonna toss on the grill."

"That sounds great for you men. I'll stop at a store on the way—I think there's one open on Tchoupitoulas Street—and pick up some chicken breasts."

"Sure, that'll be fine." My favorite, he thought, boneless, skinless white meat. "Come on over."

It was a nice party, in Tubby's cleaned-up back yard, decorated with flowers from the Green Parrot nursery which was up and running, on a warm winter evening in the City That Got Forgot. Tubby had decided to toast his suspicious oysters on the grill, and he had Steve with him outside testing them. Everybody else was in the house watching an old Clint Eastwood video. The television worked, but Cox had yet to turn the cable on.

Gastro saw something in Clint he didn't like and wandered out of the living room. Hope, who had been curious about this "boy-in-black" who kept a journal, gave him a minute or two and then followed. He was at the dining room table scratching away in a little notebook.

"What are you writing?" she interrupted.

The pen shot from his fingers and hit the floor. The notebook went into his shirt.

"I guess it's a diary," he said.

"And diaries are private."

Gastro nodded.

Hope sat down.

"Not all diaries are," she said. "A great many people's diaries have been published. Sometimes you might as well call them journals. Have you ever heard of the *Journals of Lewis and Clark*?"

Gastro admitted he had not.

"Really. They're famous around here because one of our local professors wrote about them, and of course they were exploring the Louisiana Purchase."

"I've heard of that," Gastro said. He ran his fingers nervously through his black hair.

"I'd like to read something of yours. You know, see if it's any good. I'm a teacher and I can't help being curious."

"It's mostly about the hurricane and the people I've met."

"We're all in that together, aren't we honey. Anyway . . ."

"Okay," he said eagerly, "there's something I wouldn't care if you read."

"Yes?"

Gastro retrieved his book and flipped through the pages.

"It's a poem," he explained, and shoved the bent and weather-worn pad across the cherry-wood table.

> I am warm and I am growing strong
> For your arms I am wrong.
> I am free, it's meant to be
> Hot sea
> Hot sea coming into me
> Alive and strong with jade water
> The blue sky empty of all but me
> Swirling, whirling, wetter, how much faster can I go?
> Thunderbolts hurled in all directions
> Bring the waves up to perfection
> Land and sea make our connection
> I feel like I'm getting a big . . .

"That's as far as you wrote?" she asked. "I think you've been around nothing but men for too long."

"Yes, ma'am, but I'm going to change the ending."

"To what?"

"I'm a really big creation?" he improvised.

"It shows great promise," she told him.

CHRISTINE WANDERED out in the yard. Steve had dragged a bucket of oysters over to a faucet beside the house and was washing them off.

Tubby was beside the warm grill.

"Everything all right?" she asked to start the conversation.

"Going great. Do you want to try an oyster?"

"Maybe just one," she said, and her father handed her a nice toasty, craggy shell.

"It's already opened by the heat," he said. "You can just pry it apart with your fingers."

"I know how to eat a grilled oyster, Daddy," she said. And in fact she split it open expertly and sucked out the steamed morsel within with a fine slurp. He watched admiringly.

"Ummm. Not bad," she said.

"We got lots," he told her. "I forgot you knew how to do that."

"You showed me years ago. We had a barbecue with the Fraparoules."

"I forgot about that. I'm such an old man I think I've lost track of some of the things we did together."

"You're not that old, Daddy."

Sure he was. Forty-something was old.

"How did you get to be so strong?" he blurted out.

She blushed, but he couldn't see it.

"I'm not so strong," she laughed.

"Sure you are. You went through this whole thing with that madman who kept saying his name was Katrina, and he hurt you, which makes me start to cry, and you haven't complained about it or blamed me for it . . ."

"Why would I blame you for it?" she exclaimed.

"Because he used me to get you. You were coming to try to save me."

"You'd do the same for any of us."

"Sure I would, but you're just a kid. How'd you get to be so smart that you could talk your way and fight your way out of everything he did to you, and you're still upbeat about life?"

"Daddy, I wasn't so smart or so strong, and in a way I felt sorry for Bonner."

"Get over that, please," Tubby objected.

"Maybe he could have been helped."

Tubby exploded. "If that man wanted help, he sure picked the wrong time to come to New Orleans!"

"I guess," she said. "I have thought about this a lot, and smashing Bonner on the head did make me feel a lot better personally."

"I would think so," Tubby agreed.

"I'm learning not to let things get me so far down I can't get back up again." Christine said. "A lot of it is just your attitude."

"How did you learn that?" he wanted to know.

"From you, I think. You never got too low, even when you and mom got divorced. And you took me to those jazz funerals, don't you remember?"

"I guess I did," he said, bringing back pictures from a decade before. He remembered taking his other daughters to those. Now he remembered Christine.

"That's the spirit of New Orleans, isn't it? To dance away death. To carry on with joy in the face of despair."

"Whoa, baby," Tubby exhaled.

"So I think I got a lot of my survival instincts from you."

HOPE FOUND THEM OUT THERE, staring at each other. Her arrival broke the spell. Christine went off to wash her hands, and Tubby had to mop his eyes with a paper towel.

"I guess I interrupted you," she said.

"Families, wow," was all he could say.

"It looks like you've got yours together, and some new members named Gastro and Steve."

"I don't know what to do with them all. Listen, I know I was kind of in a deep pit when I saw you the last time. I understand now why you moved out."

She laughed. "I moved out because I had to get back to my own life, but, yes, it wasn't easy to be around you."

"Maybe I'll be better. It's just that this whole city is such a damned wreck."

"You've made your own home come back. That's all anybody can do."

"But so many people aren't able to do that."

"That's true, but we've all got to play the hand we're dealt. And if we can get the politics straightened out around here, we can help everybody return home."

"That all sounds extremely pie-in-the-sky," he said, not convinced.

"That's the only way you can be. I'm already thinking about parading in Muses again at Mardi Gras this year."

"Do you think they'll have Mardi Gras?" Tubby asked, brightening. "I'm already regretting every parade I ever missed back in the old times."

"Sure we'll have Mardi Gas. We have to parade in New Orleans. It's what we do. It's our triumph over poverty and pain."

"Really?"

"I read that in a book," she said.

He took some deep breaths of cool fragrant air.

"It's a nice winter," he said.

"It's about the most pleasant I can remember," Hope agreed. "Maybe it has something to do with the hurricane."

"Everything does. I probably could have got him off."

"What?"

"Rivette. If I'd been his lawyer. Despite all he did, I probably could have got him off. Instead of that, I . . ."

"If you're interested in new cases, I heard about one," Steve said, toweling off the grill for the chicken.

"Yeah, what's that?" Tubby asked. He wasn't much interested in handling somebody's dispute with his landlord or his insurance company.

"While I was hanging with Gastro we took a walk and met a guy I know. He's a black guy and he lives by where the levee broke and flooded all the neighborhoods in our part of Plaquemines Parish."

"Okay."

"He said it wasn't just an act of nature, or anything. He called it a curse."

"Great."

"But what really caused the levee to break, he said, was the government built it over an old graveyard, so you know, like, the soil was weak and gave way."

"The Corps of Engineers put a levee on top of a cemetery?"

"Uh, huh. Years ago. And some of the big wheels down in the parish stole the land from these black people I'm talking about and sold it to the government. They even bulldozed a church."

"And the soil was weak, and the levee gave way and hundreds of homes got flooded?"

"That's what he said happened."

"And some local people got rich off the deal?"

"I don't know that many details."

"Can you find the man who told you that?"

"I guess I can easy. His name is Mister Plauche, and he lives right by my auntie's."

Tubby contemplated a budding dogwood tree, fooled into thinking it was spring. There was a sudsy beer mug in his hand.

"So that could be a good case, right, Mr. Dubonnet?"

Tubby felt the gray fog lifting, blowing away.

HE GOT A CALL LATE THAT NIGHT, after everyone had turned in, from his pal Raisin Partlow, still stuck in Bolivia.

"The whole group's okay, man? You getting it all back together?"

"Yes. Everybody's safe and accounted for," Tubby said. But then it occurred to him, he didn't know where Cherrylynn was.

"How's it going in New Orleans these days?"

"Not too bad. Katrina's gone. You ought to come back home."

"Has life sort of returned to normal?" The music in the background was salsa. Raisin was at the Russian bar, in Santa Cruz.

"After what we've been through, my friend, I don't ever want things to return to normal." Tubby said. "I don't expect a prize, but I think we deserve everything to be a whole lot better than it ever was before."

Acknowledgments

I CAN NEVER REPAY THE DEAR FRIENDS AND TOTAL STRANG-
ers who helped my family during our exodus from the storm,
a journey of many weeks across several states. Those who fed,
housed and schooled us, and offered good cheer when we needed
it most, are too numerous to mention, yet, an attempt: Special
thanks to the Mississippians, Linda and Michael Raff, David and
Whit Waide, Claiborne and Marian Barksdale, Lisa and Richard
Howorth, and Mary Hartwell and Beckett Howorth; and to the
Tennesseans, Mary Grey James, Don and Alice Schwartz, Ann
and John Egerton, Donna and Webb Campbell, Karla and Andy
Griffin, Rebecca and Joe Ingle, and "Miss (Camille) Gift." Without
the long-term hospitality of Will Robinson and Elizabeth and Jack
Wallace, I have no idea what we would have done. They gave us
the happy memories of our life on the road.